THE SIGN

Shortcut Man Novels by p.g. sturges

* * * * * * *

Shortcut Man
Tribulations of the Shortcut Man
Angel's Gate
Ipso Fatso

Other Novels by p.g. sturges

* * * * * * *

LIFE.2
Failure to Yield
The Significance of Putty

The *Significance* of PUTTY

p.g. sturges

BARKING LION

Paperback Edition:
1st Printing by Barking Lion, June 2022

ISBN: 9798806233302

Cover and Book Design: Jason D McKean

Printed by KDP / Amazon

Dedication

To my great friend, the world's greatest
conversationalist, and a damn good drummer,
Richard Christian Matheson

To my great friend, loyal, funny, brilliant
in word and deed, a true wizard,
Jason D McKean

A Note from the Author

It is not the author's intention to amend, emend, reduce, ameliorate, or redress any wrongs, misfortunes, tragedies, or perditious conditions known to exist in this world or the next. You will depart the premises no wiser than you arrived. However, it is hoped you will be entertained in the meantime.

p.g. sturges

TABLE OF CONTENTS

BOOK I
Thackeray Daiquiri

Chapter 1 – A Privilege and an Opportunity 11
Chapter 2 – Sizzler Night 17
Chapter 3 – The Encumbrance of Doctors 21
Chapter 4 – Eureka! 25
Chapter 5 – Big Breakfast 29
Chapter 6 – Declaration of Unshakable Purpose 35
Chapter 7 – Rubicon 37
Chapter 8 – Fit as a Furdle 39
Chapter 9 – Soluble Identity 45
Chapter 10 – Identity Rituals, Societal Feedback, and Emotional Punctuality 47
Chapter 11 – Free Jazz 51
Chapter 12 – Nurse Corro Taps Her Little White Shoe 55
Chapter 13 – Like a Duck 59
Chapter 14 – Stamler's Report 61
Chapter 15 – To Encourage and Re-educate 65
Chapter 16 – At Thackstone 69
Chapter 17 – Searching 73
Chapter 18 – Dr. Boother's Frustrations 83
Chapter 19 – Crustaceans and John Webster Fennis ... 87
Chapter 20 – Throw the Doc a Bone 95
Chapter 21 – Thackeray Entertainment 97
Chapter 22 – Forty-Five Minutes 103
Chapter 23 – Slow Learner 105
Chapter 24 – Grooving with the Arhats 111
Chapter 25 – A New Plan 119

Chapter 26 – The Eagle and the Dove 123
Chapter 27 – A Life of Its Own 127
Chapter 28 – At His Own Pleasure 139
Chapter 29 – Thackeray Daiquiri 145
Chapter 30 – Eleven 149
Chapter 31 – Lucky Franklin 155

BOOK II
The Patient of Dr. Singh

Chapter 32 – Artifice and Intention 163
Chapter 33 – God 167
Chapter 34 – Blue Smock and Friends 171
Chapter 35 – Dr. Singh and Estelle 175
Chapter 36 – Grigson Putty, Honest Work 183
Chapter 37 – Hunter Baldwin 187
Chapter 38 – The VTLAs 191
Chapter 39 – Hammer Up 199
Chapter 40 – Hammer Down 211
Chapter 41 – The Hollywood Sign 217

BOOK III
The Significance of Putty

Chapter 42 – The Significance of Putty 221
Chapter 43 – Quick Makes a Deal 233
Chapter 44 – Thackeray Gets It Right 237
Chapter 45 – To Illuminate the Heavens and
Warm the Feet of God 241

Epilogue 1 243
Epilogue 2 245

BOOK I

Thackeray Daiquiri

Chapter 1

A Privilege and an Opportunity

Putty. The glutinous admixture of ground chalk and boiled linseed oil. There wasn't all that much to it. Properly proportioned, 85/15, and properly mixed, it should roll freely in the hands without exuding oil. These were the simple facts of putty. And even though these were the facts in their entirety, they went far beyond what Michael Quick had ever anticipated incorporating into his body of knowledge.

Quick was forty-three years of age, and at one time, twenty years previous, it was said he held great promise. Accordingly, he had marched through life to the tempo of his own drummer. But somewhere between his second novel and twelfth screenplay the drummer quit. Leaving Quick adrift in the sea of life with bills to pay. That was when Grigson Putty, Inc. entered his life.

Lionel Grigson was now just a genial face on the wall, a relative of kindly Mary See perhaps, but his putty sealed on, here, there, and everywhere, a staple of grateful glaziers worldwide.

Grigson Putty, Inc., the enterprise to which he had given his name and his life, now inhabited a thirty-five thousand square foot single-story tilt-up on South Benner Street in downtown Los Angeles.

The bell rang. Quick shoved himself to his feet and pushed the belt into standby/non-delivery mode with the operator's button. It was ten-fifteen exactly, morning break. Fast Eddie and his roach-coach would be jouncing down the alley through the puddles left by last night's rain.

Quick stepped out onto the wet pavement. He was greeted by his friend, Clay Neff. "Merry Christmas Eve to you," said Clay. Clay was always in a good mood. He was black, sixty-three, going gray. Rumor had it he had played bass for the Chambers Brothers.

Quick looked up at the sky, threatening and heavy. It added to the attractive squalor of the alley. Wet brick buildings, sagging rusty chain-link fences, crumpled soggy cardboard boxes, broken glass, a turned-over shopping cart with three wheels. Squalor it took a writer to appreciate.

"Your screenplay sell last night, young man?" asked Clay.

Quick shook his head. Clay made the same inquiry every morning. And meant it. Quick dug through the roach-coach ice bin for a Jolt Cola. Twice the caffeine for the same seventy-five cents. A useful bargain. Clay got his daily turkey on wheat.

Purchases in hand, Quick and Clay made their way down the alley, took refuge under the awning of the non-operating emergency door. This was their usual spot from which they observed the morning theater. The theater of life.

After disposing of half of his sandwich, Clay checked his watch. "We got nine minutes, brother." He opened a huge hand to reveal a large, lumpy joint. "Pause for the cause?"

Quick usually paused, and half the time brought the materials, but every day he thought about it. Certainly the ingestion of marijuana was not recommended during working hours by the Board of Labor. On the other hand, it could not compromise his job performance. Because he had the stupidest job in the world. And good marijuana would infuse oldies radio with a little color. He pulled the lighter from his pocket, handed it to Clay.

Quick's formal job description was Enclosure Completion Technician. That is, after forty-three years of karma, dharma, exploration, invention, synthesis, good deeds, and unceasing, back-breaking effort, he now put lids on one-pound cans of putty. For a living. *For a living*. He was a "lidder."

Specifically, as a twelve-inch conveyor belt slid one-pound cans slowly past him, he checked them for acceptable volume, placed lids on them, then slammed the lids home with a mallet. He was allotted 5.3 seconds per can.

It was a job that utilized no human characteristics or capabilities. Surely, he reasoned, someone had invented a machine to replace him. And indeed someone had, but Grigson, pursuing frugality, found Quick a bargain made of meat.

Back at his task for twenty minutes, suddenly the conveyor belt stopped. Quick's mallet quivered agonizingly in mid-air. His stoned groove shattered, he looked for the source of stoppage. And there was one of the scourges of humanity, Earl Strickman, floor supervisor, finger on the conveyor belt over-ride. "Uhhh, is there a problem, Earl?" asked Quick.

"There most certainly is." Strickman vibrated with mean satisfaction. "Bud Hunt wants to see you."

Strickman, thirty-one, was paunchy, thickly bespectacled, and balding pinkly. He had a college education. He wore a wrinkly, short-sleeved white shirt and a greasy polyester-blend blue tie. He took his putty seriously. He was despised and feared.

Hunt's office was at the top of the stairs. A dirty window looked out over the alley. Hunt was a packrat.

Every horizontal surface was stacked with tottering piles of junk. The walls were hung with ancient industrial calendars. Smiling bikini-clad girls held easy-outs, rubber mats, cans of penetrating fluid, saw blades, or lifetime screwdrivers. A brace of fluorescent lamps hung from the ceiling. They buzzed and hummed.

Hunt had no neck, mean little red eyes, and a crew-cut. He was seldom seen by the troops. Quick sat in one of the two chairs set in front of the desk. "Where's Neff?" asked Hunt. At that moment Clay walked in and was gestured sarcastically to a chair by Strickman.

"So," said Hunt, "I'm told you guys think employment is a right."

Clay ascertained the lay of the land instantly. "Not a right, Mr. Hunt," he intoned with injured solemnity, "it's a privilege and an opportunity. Is there a problem?" Clay was angelic in his innocence.

"You know what the problem is," said Strickman, stonily.

Clay, bruised, looked around the room. "Has something transpired of which I'm not aware?"

"I'm told you guys were smokin' that wacky tobacky," said Hunt.

"What's wacky tobacky?" asked Clay.

"Who ratted on us? I'll kick his lying ass." Quick punched fist into palm.

"Enough of this," interjected Strickman. "You guys know what Mr. Hunt is talking about." Strickman regarded smart-ass Quick. He wasn't fooled. And Quick was no writer. Writers didn't work at Grigson.

Clay spread his huge, gentle hands. "I don't know what nobody's talkin' about."

"Either do I," harmonized Quick.

"Then why are your eyes so red, Mr. Quick?" pressed Strickman.

"I'm sorry, *doctor*, I have allergies."

"Allergies to what?" queried Hunt.

"To boiled linseed oil, ground chalk, and bullshit."

Hunt sighed. Every now and then you had to fire somebody. The exact circumstances, even guilt or innocence, weren't important. Executive action was what was important. It kept the rats in line. Let them know there were standards. Quick was an adequate lidder. But who wasn't? And Neff? Neff was a good mixer and that took a little skill. But not that much. Putty was forgiving. Hunt looked at the two miscreants. "Both of you are fired."

A slow shock wave spread through Quick, his heartbeat thudding behind his eyes. Apparently the psyche did not discriminate as to quality of the position, it reacted to dismissal itself.

Hunt amended his pronouncement. "Unless I've made a mistake and only one of you is guilty. In that case let the guilty man step forward and take responsibility." Hunt looked from man to man.

Quick turned to stare into the eyes of Clay Neff. Neff's eyes were eons deep. Like he'd seen everything. And had managed to survive.

Quick found himself on his feet. "Sorry, Clay. Didn't mean to screw you up back there. Been nice working with you." He clapped his friend on the shoulder.

Quick now directed himself to Hunt and Strickman. "It was me doing the smoking, not Clay. And actually, you guys have done me a big favor. Because my job down there was the world's stupidest job. Every time I saw myself in the mirror I would be embarrassed. If I couldn't smoke ten joints a day, I couldn't do the job at all. The better man you are, the more drugs you need. Only an imbecile could do it straight. I recommend Mr. Strickman for the post."

Quick drew his hands into one-finger salutes. "Season's greetings, gentlemen."

So ended Quick's career at Grigson Putty.

Chapter 2

Sizzler Night

Quick climbed into his white, 1969 Cadillac Coupe de Ville convertible, started it up, and eased into the riverine flow of San Julian Street. Quick loved his Cadillac. Still attractive after a hundred and ninety-seven thousand miles, it was nineteen feet seven inches long and had once been the property of a three-star general. It was a man-sized vehicle. Room for six friends, six cases of beer, and sixty kilos of fragrant Mexican green.

Even though it was Christmas Eve, it was still Thursday night, which meant Sizzler night with Estelle. She would not be pleased with the goings-on at Grigson. Actually, when he allowed himself to think about it, he had lost the power to make her happy a good while ago. But the relationship rolled forward on momentum and fear of being alone. He would hold back the Grigson news.

At Sizzler, chewing a combative little filet mignon, he watched Estelle approach with her second tray, settle into her seat, and begin sawing away.

"How's your steak?" asked Estelle, after a bit.

Quick shrugged. "It's okay."

"Just okay?"

"It's fine." Wasn't that the essence of Sizzler anyhow? Purposeful mediocrity? Okay was the business plan. "It's okay. I like the concept better than the steak itself."

Estelle grew annoyed. Steak was not a concept. It was meat. "Steak is not a concept, professor," she said, "it's meat." Another bite slid down her gullet on a bubbling river of Diet Pepsi. "What concept are you talking about?"

Quick smiled. "A concept of natural attraction to all Americans. A variation on the swindler's eternal melody, something for nothing."

"We're getting something for nothing? We're not getting something for nothing."

"Of course not. We've been promised the next best thing: a lot for a little."

"What's wrong with a lot for a little?" Estelle studied Michael's face. Her infatuation a victim of time passing, it was now clear that one of his ears sat higher than the other. Which is why his stupid sunglasses always sat crooked.

"What's wrong with a lot for a little, is that it doesn't exist." A Sizzler steak seemed like a bargain in itself. The clever part was charging for every other thing you might need besides salt and pepper. Butter pats, sour cream, chives, drink refills. Side orders or jumbo side orders for just a little bit more. By the time you got a little of this and a little of that and a little of the other, you ended up paying a lot and you may as well have gone to a good place to begin with. Like the Pantry. Or Taylor's.

"Why doesn't a lot for a little exist?" Estelle was exasperated.

"Never mind." Any explanation he might now provide would be rejected.

Estelle's eyes narrowed. Something was wrong. He was hiding something. And ruining her dinner. "What happened to you today?"

Quick sat back. Here goes. He'd put a good face on it. "Well, I'm no longer employed at Grigson."

Estelle's mouth dropped open. "What happened?"

Quick shrugged. "I guess the, uh, the Christmas putty surge failed to materialize."

"A putty surge at Christmas?"

Estelle's sense of humor was not going to wrap itself around the current situation, that much was clear. Quick sat a little straighter. "Actually, I quit," he said, with as much nonchalance as he could manage.

"Quit? You *quit?* After Uncle Roland went to Bud Hunt?"

"Yes." Even after Uncle Roland went to Bud Hunt.

Estelle wasn't taking this well.

"Yes, I quit. I'm sorry that disappoints you. I was hoping you'd be on my side. It was the stupidest job I ever had in my life."

Estelle shook her head slowly, tragically. "You *quit* your job. How will I ever learn to depend on you? When you're always quitting when the going gets tough? How will I?"

Quick judged her questions rhetorical. "You remember what I used to do all day, don't you?"

"Uncle Roland was in the containment department for eighteen years."

"I put lids on one-pound cans of putty, Estelle."

"Slow and steady wins the race."

"I'm not racing. I'm putting lids on one-pound cans of putty."

"So did Uncle Roland. And there's always room for advancement, Michael." She paused and glowered. "If you're ambitious."

Quick recalled Sun Tzu. Some battles weren't worth winning. He sat in silence.

"Well. Are you?"

"Am I what?"

"Are you ambitious?"

"Yes."

"How ambitious?"

"Uh, very ambitious."

"There's always room for advancement, Michael."

"You're right."

"I *am* right. There's *always* room for advancement."

Quick shrugged. "Uh, there're five-pound cans."

With an audible snap the camel's back was broken. Estelle pushed herself to her feet, wiped her mouth with her napkin. "Goodbye, Michael," she said. With that, she walked out, leaving him to contemplate life's rich pageant.

The man in the next booth turned around to him. "You going after her?" he asked.

Quick shook his head. "Nope," he said. "And mind your own business."

Chapter 3

The Encumbrance of Doctors

Quick was a writer and musician. Success had always seemed imminent, even as the years went by. Looking back, his efforts had been unwavering and though not crowned spectacularly, they provoked no discouragement. Which was a sign of something. Whether good or bad he hadn't figured out. But whatever it was, it was too late to turn back now.

Wives had come and gone, falling in love with the very things that later sent them screaming into the night. Estelle hadn't been a particularly good fit right from the start, but something in her smile overwhelmed his reason. He had not fallen in love. Rather, he slid into it, observing himself bemused and vulnerable, on slippery slopes.

Overwhelmed reason. Would that prove to be the theme of his life? Others accepted their limitations and modesties, but not he. Now he felt the legions laughing as he advanced to the plate, bearing the necessity of a nine-hundred-foot home run. Luckily, he mused, this was only the seventh inning.

He heard a knock at his front door. Estelle? Not likely.

He dragged himself off the couch. His unlovely apartment manager, Archie Bellrod. A dough-face. Everything about Bellrod, clothes, ideas, skin, had all gone gray. He was sixty-nine years old. "Gotta couple of packages," said Bellrod.

Bellrod was a Christian Scientist who was always

scratching, snuffling, hacking, or panting for breath. Where was the science? On the good side, he had not encumbered his life with doctors. He handed Quick two large envelopes, certified mail. "What are these, special phone books? You must have quite a collection by now."

"They're manuscripts," explained Quick. "Unpublished books."

Bellrod's rheumy eyes reflected no understanding. He wiped his nose on a finger and cleared his throat. "Them things rare? You collect'em?"

"I write them." And they return them.

Bellrod's brow furrowed with suspicion. "You write'em? I thought you worked downtown."

"I did when last we talked."

Bellrod was unfazed by the past tense. "You know what I like? Them Reader's Digest condensed novels. Y'ever read any?"

Quick shook his head. Art improved by committee.

"Try'em, you'd like'em. They're shorter than regular novels, see? They just squeeze the crap out of them. Leaving you what you need, the meat."

"You like plain meat?"

"Except when I'm eating. Then you need the fixin's." Something else occurred to Bellrod. He reached into his back pocket, pulled out a crumpled letter. "This was in the wrong box up front." He passed the envelope to Quick. "These new mailmen. I don't think they can read."

"And it's discriminatory to ask."

Bellrod shook his head. "They'll give any sonuvabitch a sack."

Of course they would. Except when you might need a sack. At twenty-one dollars an hour. At twenty-one dollars an hour, he, Quick, would gladly inform the multitudes that *this window is closed,* that *you're in the wrong line.* Or to tell others to *stand behind the rope* while he tickled his ass with his thumb. A career path, health insurance, and the thanks of a grateful nation while being rude, unhelpful, and obstructive. Who wouldn't want that?

Bellrod pointed at the letter he had just delivered. "It says it's time sensitive. Probably from an insurance company. I hate them bastards, too."

Quick nodded. "You've researched widely, Mr. Bellrod."

"I call'em spiders. *Spiders.* Bettin' against you every second from their sticky webs of sin." Bellrod coughed up some phlegm, deposited it into his handkerchief, examined the evidence, balled it up, put the handkerchief back into his pocket. "Merry Christmas, by the way. And Happy New Year."

A wave of depression came over him as he shut the door behind Bellrod. If this man were a true representative of America, Quick's life had been, and would continue to be, a hopeless campaign of providing the unpalatable for the oblivious. But it was too late to turn back now.

Chapter 4

Eureka!

Quick, long nourished on rejection, tore open the returned manuscripts with nary a hope.

Dear Mr. Quick,
Per our conversation, I am returning your screenplay, ZANEN'S GRAVE. Thanks for letting me consider it for representation. Let's keep trying!
Best wishes, Dot Hutton

Dear Michael,
ZANEN'S GRAVE! What a screenplay! The writing is stupendous, the characters enormous and interesting, the plot arresting, the climax wonderfully exciting. Unfortunately, we are not looking for material of this nature.
Best wishes, Hut Drayton

Dear Mr. Quick,
Congratulations! It is with great satisfaction that I have just finished your new screenplay, THE EAGLE AND THE DOVE. You have no shortage of brilliant, incendiary ideas! The Pope and the Dali Lama meeting in a desert roadside diner -- outrageous and utterly original! However, it is with regret that I must inform you that, presently, we have too many similar projects on the table. Let's keep trying.
Best wishes, Dray Stevens

The funny thing about it was he did keep trying. Because the ideas kept coming. While he shopped for groceries, as he watched himself with various women, as he malleted cans of putty. It wasn't ambition. It was god-given talent. And destiny. He wrote because he had to.

Television fare, sans cable, which he could not afford, was limited that night. All the channels were playing one movie, *It's a Wonderful Life*. Half were colorized, half in black andwhite. Channel Two was the banister scene. Channel Four, Mr. Potter lowered the boom, *malfeasance, fraud, misuse of funds*. Channel Seven, George was about to jump into the river to save Clarence. On Channel Nine a bell rings, another angel gets his wings.

The television oozed sugar. It was enough to drive a man to read mail from an insurance company. He picked up Bellrod's special delivery. Veteran's Life and Casualty. He was reinformed that, minus an in-convenience fee of $122.43, the sum of $31,500 would be remitted to the St. Jude's Children's Hospital upon his death, so long as he died before 12:01 am January first.

He imagined the hospital in receipt of such a check. Functionaries in Billing and Finance would accept it, someone would sign it, eventually it would flow into the general fund. Months later, after trickle-down amelioration, a sick child would get five dollars and a dry, cold, grilled cheese sandwich. The world sucked.

Back on Channel Seven, Clarence explained to George that he, Clarence, had saved George. That Clarence jumping into the river saved George from jumping in with bad intention.

It was at that exact moment that Quick experienced epiphany. What the hell was he doing? He, Michael Quick, didn't have to take shit from anyone, God included. Wasn't that the essence of free will? Quick answered to no one. Neither God nor Colonel Sanders. Even if they were the same person.

In his previous forty-three years, Quick had characterized suicide as thoughtless, ungrateful, and shortsighted. Yet now the concept of taking one's own life settled on his mind gently and logically, like a fleecy coat on a cold day. A rational solution to an irrational world. There were other rational solutions, true, like inebriation, but that was only temporary, and in the long run, ruinously expensive. Suicide was simple, certain, and serene. And cheap.

He waited for opposing thoughts to manifest but none did. What was life anyway? An unintelligible respite between voids. A frail window box of hope facing the bitter elements. A piercing shriek in a smothering silence.

His thought process moved forward. Some suicides were better than others. First, the act must be successful. Second, unambiguous. It must reflect unbending will and resolve.

And it should have, what would be the word ... *dimension.*

Like that monk in Viet Nam. Now that was suicide. Major suicide. Though fire wasn't for him. He'd burned a finger fucking with candles at his last birthday party and it hurt like the dickens.

Dimension. He needed dimension. But what kind? A protest, an excoriation, a blast of trumpets, a manifesto. Something definitely larger than himself.

His mind churned on the grist of his own extinction. Then it occurred to him. It would be an artistic protest. Against the lawyers and agents and wheedlers and moneymen who'd ruined Hollywood. The Yalies and the Harvardites who'd corrupted and debased the creative instinct. Bastards. Then the method bloomed in his mind and he was filled with a rich and pregnant satisfaction.

The Hollywood Sign! He'd hang himself from the top of the first vertical member of the letter H. A body-blow against philistines everywhere. Of course, due to universal horror and regret, his posthumous projects would achieve a ghastly fame that would flicker down the corridor of ages.

Conception, ratification, execution. All that was left was the doing. And that, as any artist well knew, that was the easy part.

Chapter 5

Big Breakfast

Normally a reluctant riser, the next morning found Quick clear-eyed and excited, brimming with life. Merry Christmas to all! The air was perfumed with purpose and charged with possibilities. Even mind-numbing Christmas music sounded fresh. He rocked to the Three Kings, the Little Drummer Boy, and José Feliciano. Against the backdrop of eternity, everything he saw had an aura of tender innocence.

The night's sound sleep did not move him from his new position. If anything, it clarified it. The transition would take place the morning on New Year's Eve so his insurance policy would still benefit the children of St. Jude's.

At the breakfast table, he compiled a list of requisites:

1. rope (40ft)
2. bolt cutters (for cutting fencing at the sign, if there was any fencing)
3. a fully spell ckecked statement of purpose
4. working knowledge of slipknots
5. distribution of worldly goods
6. final communiqués to those who might be interested

He also made a list of the music he wished to hear a final time in this life:

1. Rolling Stones, *Exile on Main Street*

2. Hendrix, *Are You Experienced*

3. Miles Davis, *In a Silent Way*

4. Eric Clapton, *Derek and the Dominoes.* The double album.

5. Allman Brothers, *Live at the Fillmore*

6. Mahavishnu Orchestra, *Inner Mounting Flame*

7. Little Feat, *Last Record Album*

8. Ravi Shankar, *Raga in Malkauns*

9. Miroslav Rostropovich, *Bach's Cello Suites*

10. Arvo Part, *Alina*

Then Quick added one more:

11. Beatles, *Revolver*

The next several days were revelations. Maybe, he concluded with sadness, character only assumed true proportion in proximity to death. A tragic comedy in itself. He felt himself become more brave, more honest. The laughter of others now bothered him not at all.

At Rock'n' Roll Denny's, on Sunset Boulevard in the guitar district, he had ordered almost the whole menu for breakfast. Short stack, hash browns, Spanish omelet, Western omelet, eggs Benedict, breakfast steak, bacon strips, sausage links, ham, fruit cup, cantaloupe, and a chocolate shake. Along with a breakfast burrito, orange juice, tomato juice, and coffee.

His Vietnamese waitress, Tam, who thought she'd seen everything, was amazed. "You more hungry man I ever see."

Other diners were also astounded. When he looked up, they all looked down. Not that he planned to eat it all. Who could? But for the first time in his life he had ordered exactly what he wanted.

Tam laid down the bill with sudden hesitation. A one-man breakfast bill of seventy-four dollars, sixty-three cents was a record here at Denny's. She could win the one-man breakfast bill contest.

Quick read Tam's expression. Of course he could pay the bill. He had just come from Washington Savings where he had liquidated his accounts. His savings account yielded eighteen dollars. A disgrace. An indictment of modern America. But his checking account was heavy, with an extra eight hundred and twenty-seven knocking around. Rent, after all, was a concern confined to the living. Halfway through figuring the tip he realized why bother. He signaled Tam.

Tam recognized trouble immediately. "You have ploblem?" she inquired.

Quick smiled, unfolded a honeybee. Let her appreciate a picture of Benjamin Franklin, the man who'd invented lightning rods and bifocals. "You have a nice smile, Tam," he said, handing her the bill, "keep the change."

"Keep change?"

"Keep change."

Feels real, thought Tam. What good fortune! I will gerbil purchase for my son and add to savings account.

Outside the restaurant, Quick found a parking cop putting a ticket under his windshield wiper.

Officer Kelly pointed at the sign with her pen. He'd forgotten to feed the meter. But so what?

One Hour Parking. 8am-6pm.

Quick shrugged. Tickets were no longer part of his world view. He picked off the ticket, crumpled it up, tossed it into the back seat, started the engine. A billow of very black smoke rose into the air. "Thank you, officer."

Officer Kelly nodded at the cloud drifting across Sunset Boulevard. "You're going to have to do something about that."

Quick should have just politely driven off but the proximity of death fueled his thirst for justice. Arco had choked a million pitiful penguins with oily sludge but who was getting a ticket? "Do something about what?"

Officer Kelly's eyes narrowed. "Do something about your unlawful emissions."

"My what?"

"Your unlawful emissions."

"You mean the smoke?"

"I don't mean your pants."

"So you *do* mean the smoke."

"Yeah."

"Yeah?"

"Yeah."

Quick considered the insults rolling around inside his head. "So, you say I'm going to have to do something about this?"

Officer Kelly was not going along with the amusement program."Yes, sir, yes you are." Officer Kelly was cold as Solomon. She removed her ticket book from her belt.

Quick delved for the last resort. "Don't give me another ticket. Please. I'm going to die next week."

"That's not my problem, sir."

"Alright," said Quick, leaning out the window, "I've tried to be reasonable. But you've made no effort to embrace our common humanity."

"Our *what?* Let me see your license."

"I'm not showing you anything, lady. And, in the absence of human fellowship, officer," Quick paused for significance, "I suggest you blow it out your ass." With that, he stomped on the gas, and with nary a glance right or left, he banged a vicious, tire-screeching U-turn across Sunset Boulevard. He lifted a finger to the symphony of horns. Using his rearview mirror, he lit up a joint. It was going to be a good day.

And so the week melted away in a series of missions and causes. He felt himself a mixture of Dirty Harry, Robin Hood, and Mahatma Gandhi. He wrote letters to the editor, boldly destroyed loud radios in quiet parks, paid old debts, spilled red paint on statues of generals, shat on the doorstep of his neighbor, the dog-owner who'd allowed Rexus to repeatedly befoul Quick's tiny patch of grass. His real character, all his life stunted by fear and self-doubt, had taken center stage.

Morning light seeped through the cracks in the blinds. He played Mick and Keith's "Torn and Frayed" for the last time, weeping as the pedal steel guitar of Al Perkins whined across the chords. It was daybreak, December thirty-first.

Chapter 6

A Declaration of Unshakable Purpose

To whom it may concern in the artistic community,

I offer this life as a warning to those losing sight of their true purpose. Life is about love and sharing. Sharing joy, sharing pain. Art is about recognizing our common humanity, accessing that joy. Recent motion pictures, like "Blood Lust III," are not examples of what makes us lovable to God and one another. Yet "Blood Lust IV" is already in production and "Blood Lust VIII" corrupts the horizon. Don't we owe each other a little more than the pursuit of filthy lucre? Isn't it time to do something meaningful while there's still time? Use your inspiration. Use it.

Good luck and Godspeed.

Michael Quick

Chapter 7

Rubicon

The 1969 Cadillac Coupe de Ville climbed swiftly into the Hollywood Hills. He would miss his Cadillac. Conveyances in the afterlife would, most probably, not be made in Detroit by Americans. He arrived at the portion of the road above the sign, parked as far off road as he could. Hollywood and Los Angeles lay before him, Catalina, unseen, in the distance.

His bolt cutters made quick work of the chain-link fencing. The Sign, a shrine, was not impressive close up. Trash on the ground and hanging in the scrubby bushes. Beer cans, cigarette butts, broken glass, and broken dreams. There'd been some partying up here. Not the optimum place to transition to eternity, but representative of humanity as it currently infested Mother Earth.

Soon he'd meet Samuel Clemens. Isaac Newton. Babe Ruth. Brian Jones. John Lennon. But first he'd see Clara. Good God, the thought of it. His heart was in his throat.

Clara. She'd gone to work one day, felt a little strange, was dead of a heart attack by noon. She'd never seen it coming. Neither had he. They'd been married seven years. He'd been adrift ever since. She hadn't read much of his work. But she didn't have to, she said. She knew it was good. You could live with someone like that. It hurt to think about her too much.

After her passing, Quick had to redefine success. Money, power, drugs, women, and recognition. Though lately he'd been thinking of redefining his redefinition.

What was the point of goals impossible to achieve?

The first vertical member of the letter "H" was where everything was going to go down. Urban legend had it that Hugh Hefner "owned" the letter in terms of sponsorship of maintenance. Sorry, Hugh. The sign belonged to artists.

Some people thought the Playboy founder a great man. Not Quick. Though Mr. Hefner had reputedly banged a thousand busty blondes in the can while watching reruns of the Beverly Hillbillies, he wasn't Einstein, McCartney, Newton, Sturges, or Martin Luther King. Just saying.

Quick looked up. Way up. The sign was about four stories high, higher than he thought. His forty feet of rope would be enough. After all, it wasn't meant to reach the bottom.

Finally at the top, huffing and puffing, Quick stood tall, master of his own destiny. He had intended to read his Declaration of Unshakable Purpose aloud, but wind conditions were not clement and he folded it away. They'd find it. He took several deep breaths. Then snugged the rope around his neck. He wouldn't suffocate. He'd pass instantly with a broken neck. Then he heard a voice.

"Hey, you. Shithead. Come down from there." A uniformed officer of some kind was waving from the weeds. "Yo, buddy. I said get your ass down from there. Now."

Quick stared down at the civic functionary in the brown orlon monkey suit. The celestial clock of universal time and experience ticked off another second. It was time. "Fuck you," said Quick.

Then he stepped into space.

Chapter 8

Fit as a Furdle

Dr. William Stevens had become a doctor for many reasons. And though he had treated his share of depressions, exhilarations, compulsions, and aversions, every now and then something novel would come up and that was why he loved medicine. The patient in the room behind him was such a case. As he explained to Dr. Clarke, Linden Thackeray had staked out undiscovered territory.

"*The* Linden Thackeray?" asked Dr. Clarke. Judy, his wife, would find this tidbit delicious.

"Yes," smiled Stevens.

"Tell me more," said Dr. Clarke.

"Well, physically, Mr. Thackeray is in pretty good shape. Considering." Stevens stroked his chin. "Strained back, sprained ankles, separated shoulder, abrasions under the chin and around the neck, contusions everywhere."

"He's lucky he can't tie a knot," said Dr. Clarke.

"Very lucky indeed. But what makes this case very interesting is his mental condition. He can't remember things."

Dr. Clarke felt himself growing annoyed. He had been summoned for this? He recalled Dr. Stevens' reputation for interest in uninteresting things. "This seems simple enough. Concussive amnesia, trauma displacement. Does he remember his name?"

"That's where this case gets interesting," said Dr. Stevens. "His own name means nothing to him.

However, he does recollect another name and a very extensive, self-consistent history to go with it."

"Ahhh," said Dr. Clarke. So who did Linden Thackeray think he had become?

Dr. Stevens checked his watch, strictly for show. He had the famously skeptical Dr. Clarke securely by the curiosities. Again he checked the time, theatrically dismissing its fictive exhortations. "Would you like to see the patient?" he inquired of Clarke. "Briefly?"

Meanwhile, in room 9612, Quick lambasted himself for his own stupidity. He looked around. Chances were he had failed in his bid for eternity. He was apparently in a private room, thick with flowers, in an expensive hospital he could not afford. And, for whatever reason, staff members had been peeking in on him. As if he were someone to be peeked at. His last memories were of a dizzying rush towards earth. Had he hurt someone? Or set in motion a chain of events that had hurt people? That might explain the interest in him. Yet none of the busybodies seemed to cast a pejorative eye. And who the hell was What's-his-name Thackeray?

Maybe he was dead, in spite of evidence, like pain, to the contrary. If this were the afterlife, though, it was sorely underwhelming. With the visual exception of his very pretty Filipina nurse, Nurse Magat, who brooked no nonsense, all things were decidedly ordinary. He had hardly expected false advertising on the golden shore, though why not, really? Wherever he was, it didn't feel much like heaven.

But could it be hell? The ingenuity of divine spirit, pissed off, was unfathomable. A third possibility entered his mind. Suppose he neither deserved the pains of hell or the pleasures ofheaven. Perhaps he had gone to Heck, where things weren't good or bad. Heck, the mildly uncomfortable destination of the mediocre.

Where weak medicine almost ameliorated minor distress.

The door opened and two doctors came in. Their expressions were kindly and inquisitive. Perhaps they hadn't realized he had insignificant insurance. The doctor he had seen before stepped forward. "Good afternoon, Linden." He indicated his companion. "This is a colleague of mine, Dr. Clarke."

Dr. Clarke nodded. "Hi, Linden. How are we feeling?"

Quick stared at them stonily. What was this "Linden" shit again? Whatever it was, everyone was in on it.

"So, how are we, Linden?" pressed the first doctor.

Quick sighed. It wasn't exactly the bud, but he'd have to nip it. "Uh, look. This 'Linden' stuff has got to stop. I have no idea who Linden is. And I don't care who he is. I've never heard of him. Now, what's the story?"

He watched the doctors exchange a meaningful glance. Then Nurse Magat came in with a tray of medications. "Time for your meds, Mr. Thackeray." She moved to the side of his bed, checked his water jug, poured some water into a paper cup, handed him two pills. Under the eyes of the doctors and Nurse Magat, Quick obediently swallowed what he was offered.

He had made the earlier mistake of asking Nurse Magat to be called by his own name. He watched her eyes grow frosty. She stamped her foot. "You are about to annoy me," she said, threateningly. "The doctors may pretend, but accept what is true. Your name is Linden Thackeray. I will call you Linden Thackeray. Don't be O.A." Which he had learned was Filipino-anagrammatic English for over-acting.

"Okay," he had replied, docile and spineless.

Dr. Stevens smiled sympathetically. "Mr. Thackeray, we're here to offer you all the help you need. That's our mission here at Cedars-Sinai."

"Good. Then stop calling me Mr. Thackeray. That isn't my name."

This time a meaningful glance was exchanged among all three medical professionals. Nurse Magat arched her perfect eyebrows and departed.

Dr. Clarke stepped closer to the patient. "What name would you prefer being called?"

"How about my own name?"

Dr. Clarke weighed a thousand preliminary diagnoses. "What *is* your name?"

"My name is Michael Quick. Michael James Quick."

"What's your birthday?" continued Clarke.

"June 4th, 1965."

"And where were you born?"

"Bremerton, Washington. Kitsap County."

The doctors nodded politely. Quick could see they didn't believe him.

Dr. Stevens decided to play along with his patient's most obvious conceit. "So, Mr. *Quick*, how *are* we feeling today?"

Quick spread his hands dismissively. "Physically, I'm sore as hell. Mentally, I'm fit as a furdle. I mean *fiddle*. I'm as fit as a fiddle." It occurred to Quick that he wasn't sure what *fit as a fiddle* really meant. Tightly strung? Well-polished? In tune? "What I mean is, I'm, uh, fit. I feel pretty good. Considering."

"Considering what?" asked Dr. Clarke.

"Considering my cuts and contusions."

Dr. Stevens steepled his fingers carefully. "Why, Mr. Quick, would a mentally fit person put a rope around his neck and jump off the Hollywood Sign?"

"I did jump off the Hollywood Sign?"

"Yes, you did," said Stevens.

Quick was greatly relieved. "Well, then that proves it."

"Proves what?"

"Proves I'm Michael Quick."

"How does it do that?"

"Because Michael Quick planned to jump off the sign. I bought the rope, I practiced tying the knot. And then I drove up and did the jumping."

The doctors didn't look convinced. "Why did you jump off the sign?" asked Dr. Clarke.

"Sometimes suicide is a rational response to an irrational world."

"And sometimes it's jumping to a conclusion."

"Exactly, doc, exactly. That's what I was doing. Jumping to a conclusion."

"Luckily you can't tie a knot," said Dr. Clarke.

"I'll do better."

Not a lot of sense was made in the discussion after that but Quick enjoyed the repartee and the attention.

◆ ◆ ◆

Three days later Quick was sick of the attention. Nurse Magat ruled his life with a tiny, iron hand. And he was tired of the doctors trying to convince him he was Linden Thackeray. The source of their mistake was beyond comprehension. If there's one thing you know it's who you are. Right?

Then, one day, out of the blue, a black man appeared with a wheelchair. Quick was rolled to the elevators, and thence to street level where a Cadillac limousine awaited.

Drs. Clarke and Stevens looked down on their departing patient. "Did you ever see any Linden Thackeray movies?" asked Stevens.

"No," said Dr. Clarke. "I'm told they sucked."

"He made a lot of them."

"Yes." Dr. Clarke nodded. "Life is like that."

Chapter 9

Soluble Identity

It took an hour for the limousine to reach north Malibu and St. Martin's-by-the-Sea. The place looked expensive. Nurses with hats bustled over green lawns and brick paths. Quick wasn't really sure how he had come to be here. He felt himself sinking into an infantile passivity.

The limousine rolled to a stop in front of the colonnaded entry. "Welcome, Mr. Thackeray," said Dr. Cutler. Cutler was St. Martin's chief medical officer.

"Thanks," said Quick.

Dr. Cutler smiled a reassuring smile at Thackeray. This was a patient he would treat himself. Thackeray was too important to leave in the hands of an eager med school grad, untested and full of the newest theoretical bullshit. Thackeray himself seemed sedated and confused. To think, this man had directed *California Rubber King*. A masterpiece.

Quick's large private room was on the second floor. It gave out on the perfectly manicured lawn and, eventually, the misty grayness of the ocean. Most of the nurses were Hispanic or Filipino, and seemed nice, but behind their professional cheerfulness he knew they were dangerous to cross.

Quick had never before considered one's sense of identity soluble. But in atmospheres of skepticism and disbelief, he now saw that softness and doubt could creep in. His in-room TV had planetary HBO and all the premium movie channels. Linen sheets suggested and welcomed his repose. A little box of See's candies sat beside his bed. Excellencies he, Michael Quick, could not possibly afford. Suppose, just for the slightest second, he *was* Linden Thackeray? Even if he wasn't. But suppose. Where had he been all this time? What had he done? Who had he done it with?

He studied himself in the mirror. There on his chin was the small scar he had acquired chasing Peter Andreone into a leper cave in a schoolyard *Ben Hur* fantasy. No. Like it or not, he was Michael Quick and sooner or later someone would present him with a huge bill and expect Michael Quick to pay it.

Nurse Corro entered without knocking. In her hand was a tiny paper cup of medications. Quick secreted them under his tongue. But then he thought what the hell.

Chapter 10

Identity Rituals, Societal Feedback, and Emotional Punctuality

There were sixty-six beds at St. Martin's-by-the-Sea. Leslie Stewart had occupied one of them for thirty-three days. She didn't feel much different than the day she had arrived. She was thirty-one years of age, a graduate of UCLA, her degree in English. She had been competing in the greater Los Angeles chess tournament when a peculiar joylessness, that had been settling on her for weeks, suddenly became very heavy and choked off all volition. It was her move. But she found herself incapable of action or speech. She just sat there. And sat there. And sat there. Finally they led her away.

And now here was St. Martin's-by-the-Sea. Her father and stepmother had dropped her off with Dr. Cutler who had promised to assign her to his most brilliant and intuitive assistant. Then Dan and Cybil retreated to Montecito where social events had been pressing.

Dr. Bouchard seemed as confused as she was. She listened to him, intermittently, with utter disinterest. On the wall behind him, a print of de Chirico's *Girl with a Hoop* fascinated her with its empathetic melancholy. Dr. Bouchard ran out of words but Leslie barely noticed. Then a tiny nurse led her to a bench out on the lawn.

Every patient at St. Martin's considered him or herself to be fully knowledgeable about other patient's pathology. It wasn't medical epiphany, it was after a while one naturally made judgments. Even if you could not summon the energy to whisper.

Lazy Whiner, Holy Baba, Two-Faced Rat, Lad Undecided, Mr. It-Was-All-A-Mistake-I-Shouldn't-Be-Here, Slutty Virgin. Leslie felt very much removed from everyone, the passive victim of a misunderstanding too pervasive to protest against.

Then, at the table next to her in the dining room, she saw a face she seemed to recognize. He'd been here a couple of days.

Chess? No. School? No. Childhood? No. Finally it came to her. He was a celebrity. A producer or an actor or something. He had occupied a box under Whoopi Goldberg on Hollywood Squares for a while. Lindsey... no, Linden. *Linden Thackeray*. A desperately unfunny writer/producer of witless, lowbrow, jigglefest comedies. What was his problem, she wondered. Leslie's brain whirred, delivered a possible trifecta. Cocaine, underage girls, and a hot tub. Ecstasy, a boy scout troop, and a desert ranch. Heroin, drowned prostitutes, shallow graves.

Her attention returned to her dinner plate. The food was good and patients usually left a little stouter, looking healthy for their various spouses and parents. As she pushed a braised carrot around she heard a voice.

"Excuse me, miss," said Quick. The girl was pretty, dark-headed.

"Y-yes?" He had probably caught her staring at him, had read her mind.

"Are you a patient here?"

That wasn't obvious? "Yes." And?

"Do I look familiar to you?"

He had caught her staring. Embarrassment. Though he looked troubled, not playful. She brushed back an errant lock of hair. "No. No, you don't."

A look of relief crossed his not-unhandsome face. "I'm so glad you said that. I'm really glad you said that." Now she remembered what she'd heard about him. He didn't know who he was, or didn't believe it or something. A real case. Nowhere man.

The man stuck out his hand. "I'm Michael," he said. "What's your name?"

She took his hand. It was warm and big. "Leslie."

"That's a nice name. There was a nice girl when I was a kid named Leslie." The man shook his head. "Never got up the nerve to talk to her." He smiled. "Why are you here?"

"Are you sure you want to ask that question?"

Quick was puzzled. Perhaps he had crossed a line in asylum etiquette. Hell with etiquette. "Sure, I do. Why not?"

"Because I get to ask you the same question."

Quick shrugged. "Fine. Why are you here?"

Leslie smiled. She found herself at ease with this man who didn't know who he was. "I got into a weird space where it seemed too much effort to think, much less move or talk." Dr. Bouchard had gone on and on and on about identity rituals, societal feedback, and emotional punctuality.

"So you stopped moving and talking."

"I stopped right in the middle of what I was doing."

"Sure." The man nodded at her. "Makes perfect sense."

"It does?"

"Been there. Did you start barking?"

"Barking? No!"

"Good. Neither did I."

Leslie's wide-eyed surprise started both of them laughing. They laughed and laughed. "You're not being fair," she said, laughing again. She studied him. "But you got past it all? The darkness? And silence?"

"I did."

"How?"

"I guess I un-disgusted myself. I don't really know. That was the problem. I was sick and tired. And sick and tired of being sick and tired. It became a real effort just to speak. At a very deep level down there somewhere, I was unwilling to go forward.

"And then one day I got up with things to do. I didn't even think about it. Suddenly I was me again. And I wondered who I'd been.

"It takes effort to move through life. Even armed with good causes and reasons. But if you're trying to sustain something artificial, eventually it becomes impossible. So, maybe I just accepted the person I actually was. Stopped seeking to please others."

"I think you may be right," said Leslie, sipping her coffee.

The man smiled at her. "So, when did you start speaking again?"

Oh, my god, she thought. She smiled at the stranger, the stranger to himself. The man who didn't know his name, a man who called himself Michael. "When did you start speaking again?" he repeated.

Leslie smiled. A happiness, unexplainable, was rising within her. "Right this minute," said Leslie, "Right this minute!"

Chapter 11

Free Jazz

Dr. Cutler sat behind his desk and smoked his pipe. As the fragrant Cavendish eddied and climbed, he re-read, for the fifth time, the Thackeray file. He had made no headway whatsoever. He wondered if he should turn him over to Dr. Bouchard. Bouchard's patient, Leslie What's-Her-Name, had just broken through a month-long wall of silence just the day before yesterday and forged new identity rituals. Which sounded like mumbo-jumbo horseshit. But it was tough to argue with success.

The door opened and Thackeray entered, took a seat. After a second Dr. Cutler thrust his papers aside, turned to his patient. "Good afternoon, Linden."

Quick nodded. "Yo."

"So." Cutler started tapping with his pen. Then consciously halted it. "Nurse Schooley. She tells me you're still clinging to your pseudo-identity."

"I object to Nurse Schooley and I further object to the word 'cling.'"

"How would you characterize it?"

"Look, doc. I know who I am. And that's that."

"And who are you?"

"Same person I was yesterday and the day before that."

"And who would that be?" asked Dr. Cutler quickly.

"Michael James Quick. Sorry."

Dr. Cutler pursed his lips. "We've got to reorient our identity rituals."

"We've got to what?"

"We have to reorient our identity rituals."

"We do or I do?" There was that tired, plural medical personality again.

"Well, uh, *you* do."

"Figures. What are they?"

How had Bouchard described it? Masks, facts, and masked facts ... and identification signposts in juxtaposition with temporary somethings or other.

"What are identity rituals?"

"Never mind," said Dr. Cutler, "just concentrate on reorienting them."

And so two weeks passed. Every day, on the veranda, Quick played a game of chess with Leslie. Every day he was crushed in a new, surprising way. But he learned new names: Morphy, Capablanca, Kasparov, Fischer.

And every day he disappointed Dr. Cutler, who tried many different techniques to bring him back into the light. Flashcards, random numbers, free association, Rorschach testing, Reichian screaming, free jazz, and finally, non-theme fingerpainting.

Today the flashcards were colored. Dr. Cutler held up a red one.

"Red," stated Quick

A blue card. "Blue."

A yellow card. "Yellow."

"What's your name?" asked Dr. Cutler quickly.

Quick was not surprised into self-revelation. "Sorry, doc. The name is Quick."

Quick felt Dr. Cutler crumple into a smaller version of himself. Quick felt a welling at the springs of regret. "Maybe tomorrow," said Quick by way of apology. Even if Cutler was aneducated boob, contact with him had built a bridge of empathy.

Dr. Cutler waved his patient out of his office. It had occurred to him, in darker moments, that his profession could conceivably be self-fulfilling hyperbole. In darkest moments, a steaming pile of ... hyperbole. That patients regained health only when they felt good and ready. Dr. Bouchard was an ass. And the worst kind of ass: a young, cocksure ass. Screw Bouchard. He, Leviah Cutler, would cure Linden Thackeray or be damned.

Chapter 12

Nurse Corro Taps Her Little White Shoe

"Checkmate," said Leslie.

Quick shook his head. What he had come to hate about chess was its uncanny resemblance to real life. You opened confidently, boldly, you slashed around audaciously. But suddenly you had a flat tire in the fast lane and it started to rain and you made for the shoulder, thickets and beer cans. Then somebody passed you, splashed you, and all was over but the shouting.

"You didn't seem to have your mind in the game, Michael." Leslie smiled sweetly.

Quick snorted. No, Leslie, you're wrong. I had it fully in the game. It just didn't do me much good. But it sure felt good to hear his own name. Especially when she said it.

Every time she said it. Geez, I really like her, he realized. She'd snuck up on him.

He remembered, early in their acquaintance, when she had asked what he wanted to be called. "Michael," he said carefully. "That's my name."

"As in the lion-hearted."

"I think that was Richard, but I'm lion-hearted, I'll give you that."

"Then that's what I'll call you."

"Thank you." He had searched her eyes but detected no sarcasm. "Do I seem nuts to you?"

"No. You seem as sane as I am."

"Thanks a lot," he had replied and they laughed all the way through dinner.

Through many dinners. Now he watched her push away the remains of her Chicken à la Malibu. He had to admit. The grub was good around here. They smiled at one another.

"I'm going to miss you," she said.

"You bet you are. I'm the only one of me around these parts." He crunched the last bit of his creme brulée.

"I'm being discharged tomorrow," she said. The words fell flatly, creating their own space and silence.

"T-tomorrow?" Tomorrow? His role was obvious. He had to be supportive. "That's great. Outa this place? You're ready. You're ready." He rubbed his hands together. "This is great. Great."

But it wasn't. It was terrible news, heavy and frightening, a sudden wound. "Kasparov, look out." He smiled a Pinocchio smile. Fixed and wooden.

In his room, refugee status fell over him. Tomorrow he would be the lonely man who didn't fit in Linden Thackeray's universe. Nurse Corro delivered his little cup of meds and departed. Out past the green lawns, in the darkness, waves crashed onto the shore, countless and unique.

If he had any balls he'd knock on her door. Tell her all he felt. Some people met in Monaco or in Paris, feeding pigeons at the Eiffel Tower. Other people met in bathrobes and wheelchairs as Xanax coursed through their veins. He could imagine the feeling of her wooden door under his knuckles. Her embarrassed surprise as she drew back the door.

He was startled by a knock on his door. It was Leslie.

She had taken his hand and he had followed her into the moonlight. After a while they stopped and he spoke. "Could I, uh, call you sometime? When I'm outa here?"

Her eyes looked softly into his own. "Would you?"

A silent shriek of jubilation strobed his soul in a blaze of joy and glory. He reached out his hand, caressed her cheek with the back of his hand. Then they kissed. Time stopped in a moment of tenderness and possibility.

Paradise was lost when a cough was heard. Nurse Corro in her little white hat. She tapped a little white shoe. It was bad business to mix graduates and lunatics.

Chapter 13

Like a Duck

Breakfast was hurried and lunch declined and suddenly there was a long black limousine in the driveway. "Do you want to meet my father and stepmother?" asked Leslie.

Quick shook his head. "No. But thank you. Not under these conditions." He explained. "I'm only going to get one chance to make a first impression. I don't want to make that first impression wearing paper slippers."

"There not made of paper."

Quick smiled. "But they're slippers. And this is St. Martin's- Bing-by-the-Sea." He helped her load her bags into the trunk of the limousine.

"I'm going to miss you, Michael."

He nodded quickly. "I've got a question for you. The duck paradox."

"What about it?"

"If it looks like a duck, quacks like a duck, walks like a duck ..."

"But you're not a duck," said Leslie, foreseeing his thrust.

"That's right. But what if I pretended? To *be* Linden Thackeray?"

The limousine's horn bleated. Leslie winced. "I say, as long as you know who you really are, do what you need to do. That's what's important."

Quick nodded. "I think you're right."

"One more thing," said Leslie.

"What's that?"

She planted a quick kiss on his lips. "Goodbye, Michael. Be well."

Twenty-three seconds later, the limousine rolled out the gates of St. Martin's-by-the-Sea and Quick was all alone.

Chapter 14

Stamler's Report

The theory behind therapeutic flashcards was this. Of course they were mundane, they were meant to be. Symbols, shapes, colors. Presuming the physical normality of the patient, the cards' utter ordinariness would eventually push the subject from the conscious to the preconscious, where a surprise question might penetrate defense mechanisms and go directly to the truth. Dr. Cutler massaged his temples. Fuck Dr. Bouchard and the politics of identity.

Today's cards were geometric shapes. A triangle.

"Triangle," said Quick.

"Square," said Quick.

"Circle," said Quick.

"What's your name?" asked Dr. Cutler, quickly.

Quick's mouth moved without sound. Then, gathering his apparently scant resources, he thrust himself to slippered feet. "My name—my name—is—*my name is Linden Thackeray!*"

"Hurray!" shouted Dr. Cutler, throwing his flash-cards into the air.

Things moved rapidly after that. Two days later Quick met with Linden's lawyer, Morty Stamler, at a picnic table on the lawn.

Quick could see the uncertainty in the attorney's eyes. "Don't worry about me, Morty," said Quick to the complete stranger. "I'm experiencing some problems but you're going to be part of the solution. Tell me about myself. As if I knew nothing."

"Okay," said Stamler, disguising his doubts. This was an unprecedented situation. Cutler had filled him in. Linden Thackeray was back. His shit was in one sack. Unfortunately, the sack was on leave.

The question was, could he, Stamler, conscientiously represent an individual who had forgotten who he was? Though perhaps forgetting who you were was a luxury. Certainly not one he, Stamler, could afford. Which clarified everything. At seven hundred dollars an hour, he would continue his good services.

"Let's see," began the lawyer. "You are a very famous and successful writer, director, producer, and actor. You're forty-three years of age. Seven years ago you won an Oscar for Best Original Screenplay."

"An *Oscar?*" He had won an Oscar and forgotten? Good god. Perhaps it had been for *The Eagle and the Dove.* A consummate work of art, reviled multiple times by the philistines. Which is what made them philistines. "For which screenplay did I win?"

"Bubbles in the Tub."

"Bubbles in the Tub?" He'd never heard of *Bubbles in the Tub.* "What was the subject matter?" Maybe, in a special light-hearted mental state, he had renamed something with natural heft.

"It's about flatulence," said Stamler. "Then came *Too Pooped to Pop, Bikini Tiger,* and *California Rubber King.* All very well-received at the box office."

A cold sweat started in at the roots of Quick's hair and seeped down into his soul. *California Rubber King.* What in hell was that about? He had never heard of these efforts, much less written them. Flatulence?

Michael Quick had sought to challenge the Bard himself, toothless and over-rated though he was. What world was he in now? Unless he were truly ill. Perhaps Linden Thackeray was the tiny portion of himself not consumed with disease. He had to count it as a possibility.

Stamler looked through some papers, looked up. "And you're worth somewhere in the neighborhood of twenty-three million dollars. Give or take one or two."

"Twenty-three million dollars?" A weight he had never known he carried slipped off his shoulders and a slow, narcotic exhilaration slid up his spinal cord. Who was Michael Quick after all? "*Me?* I'm worth twenty-three million dollars?"

Stamler watched shock sink physically into his client. Seldom had he the opportunity to deliver unadulterated glad tidings.

"You have two homes. One in Beverly Hills, your chief residence, called Thackstone, and a condo overlooking Central Park in Manhattan. You have a penthouse in perpetual reservation on the beach in Maui. You own your own production company, Thackeray Entertainment. You have one hundred and sixty employees and nine projects in the works."

"One hundred and sixty employees." Good god. He was important. *He was important!*

"Speaking for your staff, in Beverly Hills, they're all very anxious to welcome you home."

Quick spread his hands. Why put off the inevitable? "I'm ready to go home, Morty."

Stamler extended a hand. "Welcome back, Linden."

From his office overhead, Dr. Cutler looked down on his departing, Academy Award-winning patient, Linden Thackeray. "The problem with identity rituals, Dr. Bouchard," intoned Cutler gravely, "is that they ignore subconscious representations and give rise to polycentric eccentricities. And they are, as you know, undesirable. Hence, the use of cognitive surprise mechanisms."

Dr. Bouchard nodded. It sounded like a load, but maybe it wasn't.

Chapter 15

To Encourage and Re-educate

The Santa Monica Freeway ground eastward at its customary glacial pace. Quick, ensconced in the back of a Cadillac Fleetwood Limousine, paid the traffic no mind. He had only ridden in a limousine once before. Steady Eddie, a friend who worked at Poquito Mas, had secured a second job cleaning limousines at night. They had taken the Titanic model out for a spin and a cheeseburger and had knocked over a mailbox.

Quick sniffed the stopper from an expensive-looking decanter. Maybe it was brandy. There were four TVs around the cabin. All inoperable. Until he found the remote velcroed to the ceiling. Talk about class. He aimed and clicked. On came NBC local news at noon.

Saul Croyer, the professionally affable anchor, handed off to Heidi Hogan, entertainment maven.

"Thank you, Saul," smiled Heidi. "I'm Heidi Hogan and this is Hollywood Lowdown Minute."

Heidi was a public miracle of reconstructive science. Her nose had been whittled, her lips had been fattened, her eyes had been lifted, her face had been tightened, repaved, and botoxed.

Her hair had been teased, whipped, burned, and crusted into a fearsome, immovable blond helmet. Her breasts had been inflated, raised, separated, and renippled, her cleavage now deep and contiguous. Quick had always loved her.

Heidi looked into the camera and stretched the corners of her mouth into a smile. "Today's big story is good news. Writer-director Linden Thackeray has been released from St. Martin's-by-the-Sea where he has been recuperating from a bizarre accident at the famed Hollywood sign. Thackeray was reportedly scouting locations for his new film, Bubbles III, *Bubbles in the Tubbles,* when he fell from the sign. I'm Heidi Hogan and that's all for the Hollywood Lowdown Minute."

Twelve miles away as the crow flies, at Linden Thackeray's Beverly Hills estate, Dr. Ethan Boother briefed the residents of Thackstone on the likely trials of the days ahead. "Mr. Thackeray is and will be, for some time, a frightened individual. Contrary to the reports we all have heard, he's not a well man. He's trying to *put on* his life as a man might put on a suit of clothes. His amnesia is profound and widespread. But Dr. Cutler, from St. Martin's, assures me Linden is up to, and willing to do, the hard work necessary to achieve substantial recovery. Dr. Cutler has been utilizing cognitive surprise mechanisms with Linden and has been quite encouraged by the results."

"What are cognitive surprise mechanisms?" Of all the people who lived at Thackstone, only Ginger Alford didn't receive a salary. She was Linden's girlfriend. Dr. Boother stroked his chin. "Cognitive surprise mechanisms ... cognitive surprise mechanisms are ... uh, they're unexpected phenomena, uh, utilized for exploratory purposes of, uh, exploration." He should have paid a little more attention to that windbag Cutler.

"But they've done him some good," Ginger stated hopefully.

"Enormous good." Whatever they were. Dr. Boother shifted his weight, eyed the cook and the butler. What had they understood of his extemporaneous explanations? Did they secretly think him an ass?

Mrs. Alvarez, the cook, and Bertrando, butler and

driver, were neither hot nor cold, neither curious nor incurious. They had been summoned and would remain until dismissed. Mr. Thack would still need to eat, dress, and go places regardless of the condition of his brains.

"Does he remember anything at all?" Ginger was worried. Even though the cognitive surprises were apparently promising. If she had been reduced to a total stranger she could see that her days might be numbered. Which would be a setback.

Ginger was a knockout. She would inspire anyone to remember, thought Dr. Boother. Or even to coolly fabricate. "Linden recalls historical events and personalities. He knows who the president is.

"But personally," questioned Ginger delicately, "he doesn't know anyone?"

"He didn't seem to know Morty Stamler." Boother made positive eye contact with the troops and conveyed sympathy to Ginger. "Our job is to encourage and gently reeducate. To prepare his favorite foods, to play his favorite music, to recall joyful, personal interactions. Do I make myself clear?"

Ginger nodded, knowing what she would have to do. Mrs. Alvarez and Bertrando, however, moved not a muscle. Dr. Boother couldn't tell if they'd understood a single thing. "Maybe you could lay out his favorite pants," he added, trying to get a response from Bertrando.

The butler/driver didn't even blink, just stared back at him, blank as a lizard.

Behind those lizard eyes Betrando's policy was to never let extraneous people, especially white people, corrupt his chain of command. He knew Mr. Thack was the boss. That was Plan A as far as he was concerned. The alpha and the omega. Departures from the plan meant misunderstandings, needless complications, and extra work. You could not serve two masters. Bertrando found no call for rudeness. Chain of command interlopers were wordlessly stared at until they went away.

"Well, that's it," said Dr. Boother, rubbing his hands. He needed some air.

Chapter 16

At Thackstone

The limousine crossed into Beverly Hills. Quick had always felt uneasy in Beverly Hills. The police were lackeys of the rich and idle and dispensed unequal justice accordingly. Even embraced by what must have been Corinthian leather, Quick felt apprehension at the sight of a motorcycle officer.

Officer Hendricks switched on his siren, pulled ahead of the limousine and lit up a battered, smoky, 1993 green Pontiac.

The limousine changed lanes to give the officer plenty of room. As they passed the slowing Pontiac, Quick looked over in brotherhood and sympathy. The driver raised his middle finger in reply.

Well, fuck you, ingrate, thought Quick. You don't drive pieces of shit like that in Beverly Hills. Anyone could tell you that.

The limousine turned left, climbed into the hills, and finally paused before a vast iron gate. Above the gate, letters arched the span in floral, iron cursive: *Thackstone*. Linden Thackeray was home.

Thackstone was the largest single residential structure Quick had ever laid eyes upon. Three sprawling stories of weathered brick, mullioned windows, and climbing ivy. Eight or nine people stood on the front steps gazing in his direction. Each would be disguising his or her pity and curiosity. An Hispanic man broke ranks and moved toward him.

Bertrando took one close look at Mr. Thack and

knew the Mr. Thack he had known was gone. A pity. But he would forge a useful relationship with the new Mr. Thack. After all, the new Mr. Thack was just another white man.

The meeting with the rest of the staff, residential and non-residential, was stiff and perfunctory, utter strangers imitating previous intimacies. The cook, the butler, the ophiologist, the maids, the gardeners, the maintenance men, the security team. Then, hanging toward the rear was a mismatched couple, a diffident, wispy-headed man with an absolutely gorgeous blonde-headed woman. Much too beautiful for the wisp. Quick didn't understand them or couples like them. Perhaps wisp had a purse like Gates and a cock like Man-o-War. Shallow bitch.

Unfortunately, Quick's personality congealed in the presence of beauty. It left him dull, vague, and ordinary, exuding the distracting scent of apology. Wisp stuck out his hand. He was wearing a stethoscope. Oh. That made him a doctor.

"Hi, Linden. I'm Dr. Boother. I'll be in residence until your recovery is complete. Welcome home."

"Thank you," said Quick. He realized the beautiful blonde was staring at him. He turned, looked into her eyes, held her gaze. The mutual examination went on several seconds past normal. Like a movie when the hero meets the girl. Maybe his fly was open. It wasn't.

Boother watched both of them, Thackeray opaque and Ginger distressed. If only he, Empathetic Boother, could comfort her. Boother's voice eased down into a therapeutic syrup. "Linden, this is Ginger." The doctor paused in envy. "Your girlfriend."

Were there any doubts about Thackeray's incapacity, they were erased in that moment. Quick's jaw dropped down onto his chest and he gasped like a fish.

And he instantly intuited the dark designs of Empathetic Boother. Quick lowered head into hands, as if reflecting, then raised his head and pointed in an executive manner. "Boother, make me some coffee."

He turned to Ginger. "Ginger, darling. I get the pleasure of falling in love with you all over again. God is great. But also, I'm going to make some mistakes and I ask you now to forgive me in advance. I'm going to need all the help you can spare." It was a strong finish.

Little in this world is as flattering as a powerful man requesting your assistance. Ginger sighed, a hand falling over her heart, her position threatened, but presently under favorable stars.

Boother turned for the kitchen and Quick surveyed his unlikely prize. "Shall I show you around?" asked Ginger.

"Please," said Quick.

After a brief sweep through the more public rooms, they went upstairs. "This is the master suite," the bombshell explained, with a wave of her perfumed wrist.

It was a vast, off-white sanctuary. The bed was the size of a competition trampoline and overlooked a verdant glen which came with its own babbling brook. The carpet, jade green, was as soft as a dream and stretched a full forty feet, through tasteful islands of comfortable furniture to built-in cabinets with bookcases above. Apparently, he was well read. Twain, Mailer, Musil, Wolfe, Heinlein, Asimov, Matheson, *père* and *fils*, Bradbury. With a predilection for sci-fi.

"I've really missed you, Linden," said Ginger, softly. "I'm really glad you're back."

Quick looked into her blue, blue eyes. If only he were a closer. Though artists were rarely businessmen. Yet, unsummoned, Ginger stepped nearer. Her voice fell into a moist whisper. "You don't remember anything we ever did together?"

"I wish I did," said Quick, pitifully. This was beyond all his hopes and dreams. Ginger advanced another step. Then she reached with both hands to hold his face, kissing him tenderly on the lips. The kiss grew mutual and fulminated in intensity, her bounteous bosom crushed against his chest. The kiss might have gone on forever had not Quick felt a tug at his belt.

It was not until the second tug that he realized this was no mistake. God was indeed great. One of the most elusive of all sexual phenomena was to be visited upon him right there and then.The UBJ, the unsolicited blow job.

Almost mythical, rare-as-hen's-teeth, nirvana on the mountaintop. He was filled with a deep and poignant gratitude. Ginger proved to be conscientious and adept. A minute later Quick was robbed of all strength.

He drifted into a gentle slumber and awakened later with barely a bump on the shores of consciousness. Ginger smiled down at him. "Now do you remember?" She giggled.

Quick looked into her blue, blue eyes. "Almost," he said. "Could we try it again?"

Chapter 17

Searching

The next day Quick rose to a perfect day. It took a year-round Los Angeles resident to recognize the specialness. It was a day content with itself, neither looking forward nor harkening back. It was a day that came along once or twice every year or two. The wind was an occasional baby's breath that served only to stir the stillness. Traffic flowed quietly, at reasonable pace, and in the soft sun, birds twittered from trees and powerlines, cats watched lazily from doorsteps.

Yet Quick was utterly and completely miserable. Ginger had proved imaginative and indefatigable. The six-car garage sheltered a Rolls, a Ferrari, a big Mercedes and some motorcycles. His refrigerator was a stainless steel colossus so modern he was unable to effect means of entry. His library comprised five thousand leather-bound volumes and a collection of antique telescopes and armillaries. So that's what the word meant. He'd never known with certitude, but he'd assumed an armillary a lizard of some sort. It wasn't.

But these surprises were forgivable. Worse was the return of his deep personal confusion. Michael Quick, unimpeachable witness to himself as the central character of his own life, was shaken and beleaguered. The conspiracy was too wide. And the logic of conspiracy was cumbersome and strained, right down to his fingerprints. Absolutely identical. Who would go to the trouble and why?

Perhaps he really was Linden Thackeray. Perhaps

he had done all these things, affected these many lives. Was it possible that the persona of Michael Quick was a dream born of fever, a desperate response to intolerable pressure?

Mrs. Alvarez made him a delicious breakfast which he barely tasted. He paid her profuse compliments and fled for the bedroom. Underneath the base of his bedside lamp was a phone number. Leslie's number.

He borrowed a puzzled Mrs. Alvarez's old blue Toyota and drove to Norm's Restaurant on La Cienega, found himself a booth facing the street, stared out at the street scene. He studied his reflection in the window, tapped the glass just in case it wasn't there.

He heard a voice behind him and there was Leslie. Her smile lit up her face, lifted his mood. She sat down in the orange booth. "What a beautiful day."

And he realized it was. It was just confusing as all hell. But his happiness in her presence was not confusing.

"How's your new life?"

"I'm a rich and successful man."

"Congratulations."

"Thank you."

"How big is your house?"

"You mean my estate."

"How big is it?"

"Eighteen rooms. Six baths. A six-car garage. A billiard room. A library. A screening room. And I'm told I have a bowling alley in the basement. Along with an archery range and an endless pool."

"Well, do you or don't you?"

"Don't I what?"

"Have a bowling alley and that other stuff."

"I may have."

"You *may* have."

"The basement has three levels and I keep getting lost and ending up in the snake room."

"The what room?"

"The snake room."

"The *snake* room? What's in it?"

"Snakes."

Leslie shivered. "Uggghh. Snakes. I feel filthy."

"They're clean animals."

"What do you know about snakes?"

"I dunno. A little bit."

"Nothing, in other words."

"Well, uh … not much."

"Nothing."

"Okay."

"Don't ever take me to the snake room."

"I'm not sure I could find it again."

They both laughed. Leslie searched his face. Then she tapped her temple. "How are things?"

Quick spread his hands. "I may not be Michael Quick after all."

"That happens."

"It hasn't happened to me before." He pointed to a scar at the base of his left thumb. "I used to believe I had done that laying carpet. But now I don't know." He distinctly remembered the incident. He had been working as part of an apartment complex maintenance crew. Working on his hands and knees, he'd put his hand down on a piece of glass they hadn't swept up.

Over the meal a plan was conceived. They would visit Quick's old apartment in Hollywood. This would pretty much prove things one way or another.

Coming up on Highland, they drove east on Hollywood Boulevard. Past the cheap electronics stores, manmade shoe emporiums, T-shirt and trinket shops, past Supply Sergeant. Then up Ivar. He half-hoped it wouldn't be there, but there it was, Sandwood Court. Which meant his residence at Thackstone was fraudulent. And there was someone sweeping the walkways. That would be Bellrod.

Quick parked the Toyota and they walked back to the Sandwood. Mr. Bellrod had been working hard, apparently. The place looked a little cleaner, the bushes trimmed a little better. Leslie looked up at him, he nodded. "This is it." He pointed to his door. The screen door had been fixed. Bellrod would be pissed about the rent. He'd missed one payment.

"Howya doin', Mr. Bellrod," said Quick, with a proactive joviality.

The man turned around, but it wasn't Bellrod. "Can I help you?" said the man, leaning on his broom.

"Mr. Bellrod around?"

"Maybe," said the man, lighting up a cigarette. "Who is he?"

"He's the manager here."

The man spat a speck of tobacco from the corner of his mouth, studied Quick. "I'm the manager here. Can I help you?"

"What happened to Mr. Bellrod?"

"Never heard of him. This is the Sandwood Court."

"Of course, it's Sandwood Court." Quick pointed to 1733 5/8." And that's my apartment."

"My name is Foster," said the man, glancing at Leslie to determine her place in the drama. "I've been the manager here for six years." He looked Quick up and down. "What, exactly, is your relationship with Miss Poplinski?"

"Who?" asked Quick.

As if arranged celestially, the door to 1733 5/8 opened. Raised voices were heard. An acoustic guitar sailed out the door and landed on the sparse lawn with a sad *bong/twong*. Its owner quickly followed, picking up the instrument tenderly. Miss Poplinski made her appearance in the doorway. She was a formidable woman. Twice the size of the departing musician, she stood, hands on hips. "Alice's restaurant, hotel, laundry, sex, and mothering service is now out of business. Don't come back, fucker."

Fucker slunk off, cursing under his breath. Everybody watched him go. Then Alice noticed she was under observation. "What the hell do you want?" She eyed Quick and Leslie with malevolent suspicion, turned to Foster. "You tryin' to rent this place out from under me?"

"You know her?" whispered Leslie, eyes wide.

"Never seen her before."

"She's not your wife or something?"

"No. She's not anything." Quick addressed angry Miss Poplinski. "Excuse me, ma'am, how long have you lived here?"

"Who the fuck wants to know, cowboy? You work for the government? I got my rights."

"She's been here a year and half," said Foster. "What do you need?"

Quick spread his hands. He didn't know what he needed. Against all odds, seemingly, he was, indeed, Linden Thackeray. Which meant that his residence at Thackstone was legitimate. It also meant that dearest Clara, seven years late and lamented, was a figment of his imagination, a cerebral microvoltage barking up the wrong neuronic avenue. "I'm trying to track down an old friend."

Quick and Leslie had turned for the street when Miss Poplinski's voice stopped them. "Hey, buddy, want to buy a surbahar?"

Quick stopped in his tracks. Here was a novel set of

syllables. A surbahar? What was a surbahar? A vehicle? A service? A weapon? A kitchen utensil?

And so goodbye to Sandwood Court. Next stop, Grigson Putty. Which would be the last stop on the reality train.

"What did you do down here again?" inquired Leslie. Downtown industrial Los Angeles was new to her. Depressingly grungy. Derelicts staggered around pushing shopping carts, eyes peeled for grains of hope.

"I put lids on one-pound cans of putty." He could feel Leslie's eyes boring in to the side of his head.

"That's what you did? That's all you did there?"

"Sorry. That was it."

"Some job."

"It wasn't my vocation. It was a job."

"Some job," she repeated.

He recognized no one at Grigson and no one recognized him though all the smells were familiar. He was confused with a client who had ordered several boxcars of putty. "My name is Linden Thackeray," Quick finally explained, "I'm a motion picture director."

"What do you want all that putty for?"

"I don't want it."

"How much *do* you want?"

"None of it."

"Then you've come to the wrong place."

"No, I haven't."

"Why are you here then? Scouting locations?"

"Actually," Quick began, "I had a friend a long time ago who worked here."

"What was his name?"

"Michael Quick."

The foreman, who had introduced himself as Bert Frunk, shook his head. "Not since I been here. And that's seventeen years." Frunk cupped his hands, lit up a

Marlboro. Then, coincident with the intake of tobacco, came revelation. Frunk pointed at Quick. "Wait a second. Wait a second. You said Linden Thackeray. Isn't that what you said?"

Quick nodded.

"Yeah, yeah, yeah. *Bubbles in the Tub*, right?"

"That would be me," said Quick.

"One of the all-time greats," continued Frunk. "An out-n- out fart-fest. But a fart-fest with feelings. Congratulations."

Quick signed several autographs on the way out, including one for the new lidder whose name was Pelkin. "Actually, this is just my day job," said Pelkin. "I'm really a writer."

"Good luck," said Quick.

"Maybe I could send you a script," said Pelkin.

Quick and Leslie rode in silence. Finally, passing out of downtown, speech returned. Leslie looked at him. "You had Pelker's job?"

"Pelkin."

"He was a writer, too," said Leslie.

"That's what he said." A deeply wretched co-incidence. "Maybe I didn't have that job," said Quick. "Let's talk about something else."

"Anything else," said Leslie, gratefully. "Tell me about the people at your house."

"You mean the ones who live there."

"I don't care about the mailman."

No, you care about me, thought Quick. This was the time to lean over and kiss her. But he hesitated a second and then they passed a bum on the corner shouting about Jesus Christ and the moment was lost.

"Maybe he's thinks he's John the Baptist," said Leslie.

"Maybe he *is* John the Baptist."

At Sixth and Oxford a man in a bear suit waved a sign about condominiums. "So, tell me about the pretty maids Linden's been screwing."

Quick suppressed a guilty urge to candor, reliving Ginger's tug at his belt. "There are no pretty maids. Mrs. Alvarez is fifty-six and happily on the enchilada diet."

"But what?" Leslie was expert at reading faces.

Now the kissing moment was far downstream. "But, uh, nothing," said Quick. "Nothing really." Of course, nothing is as something as *nothing really*.

"What kind of nothing really?" asked Leslie.

Quick had to think fast. Which was something he was not particularly adept at. To deny Ginger's existence would only set up ungainly ramifications later. It wasn't as if he could just throw Ginger out. He could, but it didn't sit right. Best to introduce Ginger now. Partially. "I, uh, inherited a girlfriend, uh, so to speak."

"A girlfriend?"

"Kind of. Uh, what is her name?" Quick screwed up his face, feigned searching his memory. "Uh, *Ginger*. That's it. Ginger." He paused, tried to twist his face into a countenance of passive neutrality.

"Ginger?" Leslie's enunciation was clinically precise and frigidly cold. "You have a girlfriend named Ginger and you don't remember her?"

"Well, I mean it was awkward. You know. A little. Here's a total stranger staring at you. And, uh, she can remember, I guess, things I must have done but didn't do. If you know what I mean."

"I know exactly what you mean." Leslie's eyes betrayed no warmth. "Sounds like she's hot."

Hot. *Fuck*. Somewhere he'd fumbled and managed to open the proverbial can of worms. "She's, uh, not unsightly."

"Hmmm," said Leslie. "I wouldn't want to come

between you and Ginger if there's something there."

"There's nothing there, I assure you."

"She lives at your house?"

"I believe so."

"So do I."

"Uh, uh, what I meant was . . . as far as I know she does."

"She's always there ..."

"Seemingly."

"Morning, noon, and night."

"Apparently."

"Apparently."

"You're making a bigger thing of this than it is."

"You don't take her to the snake room?"

"She doesn't like reptiles. There's nothing to worry about."

"Why would I worry?"

"I was just saying."

"Then don't."

"Leslie— ..."

"You're being very presumptuous, Michael."

Quick gave up, threw up his hands. "I give up. A girl named Ginger lives at the house—."

"Apparently."

"—so does a doctor, a cook, a butler, and some other people. I have an ophiologist in three or four times a week, too. When do I see you again?"

"What's an ophi—what did you say?"

"An ophiologist."

"What's an ophiologist?"

"A fancy name for a snake charmer."

"Yuck."

They had arrived back at Norm's. She leaned over, kissed him on the cheek. "Nice to see you, Michael. I have a tournament coming up. Why don't you come?"

She smiled and golden light filled his world.

He leaned to kiss her on the lips. It was short but very, very sweet. Then they parted.

Chapter 18

Dr. Boother's Frustrations

Quick drove back to Thackstone in a ruminative mood. Unless the victim of a celestial prank, he was a certifiable loon. He stopped at a red light on Sunset Boulevard. But was it really red? Was it really a stoplight? Was he really on Sunset? In Los Angeles? Maybe he was a potted plant, tended by Carlos Casteneda, dreaming a vegetable dream on some southwestern windowsill.

"Hey, fuckface," said a man looking over from a green Buick, "stay in your own lane." The light changed and the Buick disappeared in a cloud of black smoke.

Two weeks quickly passed, the days finding a comfortable rhythm. He talked to Leslie, very pleasantly, every day.

On a whole other plane was Ginger. He had become very fond of her. No moment seemed inopportune for a tug at the old belt. He had also taken a genuine liking to the staff. No matter what game he played with them, cards, pool, ping-pong, croquet, or a round on his backyard putting green, he always won. Or, more truthfully, they always lost.

Everyone loved Mr. Thack with the exception of Dr. Boother. Boother sat poolside, drumming his fingers on the table where the untouched morning repast was laid out. In the pool, his patient thrashed noisily to complete another lap.

Boother called to him, anxious to begin the day's therapy, but the water-clumsy, egocentric amnesiac pushed into another transit of the half-Olympic sized pool. Boother swallowed his annoyance. He was very well paid for what he considered babysitting, but, certainly in medical school he had hoped for medicine closer to the cutting edge. Aggravating his annoyance was the fact that vacuous Thackeray possessed the lovely Ginger. Boother was smarter, harder-working, better read, and had answered a higher calling in life. Yet Ginger was apparently oblivious to his superiority.

Quick pulled himself out of the pool, grabbed a towel. Prior to his recovered life he had never known towels like these. So thick, so fluffy. They rendered his past towels cheesecloth. No wonder he had always felt damp.

He sat down at the table, started lifting silver lids. Bacon, sausages, hash browns, fruit plates. A carafe of fresh-squeezed orange juice, a pot of good, strong Columbian coffee.

Dr. Boother took up a piece of honeydew melon. "Well, Linden, it's been two weeks now. How are we feeling?"

Quick drained his tall glass of orange juice. "We've never felt better, doc. Never better." He eructated loudly and longly, enjoying Boother's discomfort.

"And how do you feel your reorientation is coming along, Linden?"

In other words, how Linden-like did he feel. Quick speared a sausage link, conveyed it to his plate. "Every day I feel a little more comfortable, a little more at home." A little less likely he would be arrested for felonious impersonation.

The truth was that while he believed, intellectually, he was probably Linden Thackeray, emotionally, he still felt like Michael Quick. Fingerprints, photos and all other evidence to the contrary. "More important," continued Quick, "is how *you're* feeling, doc. How are we treating you around here?"

Quick had seen that questions about the doctor's state of mind upset the doctor/patient paradigm, and to that degree he enjoyed asking them.

"What I was saying, Lind—"

Quick broke in. "And how's our digestion, doc? I can ask Mrs. Alvarez to whip up some of that wheat-grass oatmeal." Which tasted like gopher-adulterated lawn clippings.

"Linden, it is your health that is important here."

"It better be."

"It is. So when I ask you—"

"Like I said, doc, every day we're a little more at home here. The chow is outstanding, the pool is terrific, and our people, including you, are generally fantastic." And Ginger could suck the chrome off a trailer hitch. Quick poured himself another glass of orange juice. From Valencia. *Valencia oranges*. Who knew? "Another hit of the OJ, doc?"

"No, thank you, Linden." Boother swallowed his annoyance, studied his patient. "What we're looking for, Linden, and expecting, during reconstruction, are unusually strong emotional reactions to various articles and situations. A snatch of a song, a photograph, a perfume, something like that. A street corner, even."

Quick dug a butter knife into the Dundee marmalade. You had to hand it to the Irish. They had a handle on the marmalade. And the whiskey.

He spread a generous orange glob on the sourdough toast. He looked up at the doc. "I find this marmalade unusually good." Quick paused. "Of course, I don't have your education."

No, you don't, thought Boother, trying not to grind his teeth. "Let's say you pick up a watch, for instance, and you feel a flood of sadness—or of happiness for that matter. Has anything like that happened?"

"No. But I've felt admiration."

"Admiration?"

"Deeper than that."

"How would you classify it?"

"I think I'd call it deep admiration."

"That's a start." Boother bit his lip. "For whom or what did you feel this admiration?"

Quick fingered the towel on the arm of his chair. "For this."

"For the *towel?*"

"That's right. But this is not just any towel. I think these are Egyptian cotton. Or Serbian cotton. They're really fluffy. I mean *fluffy*. Is that what you're talking about?"

"Not exactly, Linden." Thackeray was an imbecile. Perhaps even a moron. Which, sadly, made Ginger an imbecile-lover. A moron-seeker. Well, she'd found one. But what in god's name did she see in him? Besides the money. Maybe he was hung like Man-o-War.

Boother inhaled, exhaled. "In any case, Linden, strong emotional transients suggest a return to psychological normalcy."

Quick slid another sausage down his throat. "Don't worry, doc, we haven't had any transients."

"Let's not give up, Linden."

"We won't, doc, we won't." Quick didn't hate Dr. Boother and didn't want him to go away. In times of uncertainty, it was nice to have someone around who could write prescriptions.

Mrs. Alvarez came out with more coffee and Quick decided on New Zealand lamb for dinner.

Chapter 19

Crustaceans & John Webster Fennis

The following Friday night found Ginger and Quick out on the town in the big Mercedes. Ginger was still under the impression that she was his girlfriend and Quick hadn't found the heart to tell her otherwise. He suddenly recalled a showbiz establishment he had never been able to afford. The Palm. Famous for its lobster. Well, now he could afford it. "I have an idea," he said, "how about some crustaceans at the Palm?"

"I'd prefer lobster if it's all the same to you."

"Uhhh … it's exactly the same to me."

"Great. Let's do that instead."

So Quick turned off Sunset at Doheny and rolled smoothly down to Santa Monica Boulevard. Ginger put a beautifully manicured hand on his thigh. "You've been so sweet to me lately. And so manly. They should call you Tiger."

There exists nowhere a man who finds the appellation, *Tiger*, objectionable. Quick shrugged carelessly. "I've always been a manly man."

"Don't I know it. I knew Dr. Boother was wrong."

"Really. What did he say?"

"That you'd probably be very busy finding yourself. Too busy, if you know what I mean."

"I see. What did you tell him?"

"I told him when you finally found something you seemed to know what to do with it."

Boother was a low-down, back-stabbing snake, Quick had known that from the beginning. And Ginger was an eel. What did *finally* mean? What had he *finally* found? Michael Quick knew his way around in the dark. Perhaps he had discovered the El Dorado of female geography, the G-spot. It was up there somewhere. Or it wasn't. Had the G-spot been reclassified as an urban myth? It didn't matter. He could retrace his steps if necessary, let his fingers do the walking.

And here was the Palm.

After leaving the Mercedes with the grateful valet, Quick took Ginger's arm and entered the venerable eatery.

So this was fame. He felt himself emanating a soft golden light, reflected in widespread smiles and sparkling eyes, in fragrant whispers behind hands and expressions of delight and welcome. They were led, he surmised, to his favorite table. "Your favorite table, Mr. Thackeray," bowed the maître d', with professional unction.

"I'm back," said Quick, smiling, a grandee at leisure.

"We missed you greatly, sir," said the maître d', amazed at his good fortune. He turned and signaled across the room to the bartender. In two shakes of a lamb's tail drinks were delivered.

The server set them down with a flourish and hovered in fretful anticipation. These must be special drinks, thought Quick. Probably his favorite. Quick sipped the unknown libation. *Ugghhh.* Whatever it was it was dreadful. Quick pursed his lips, nodded. "Remarkable," he said, savoring the ghastly fluid. Drano on the rocks.

He ordered the lobster, large. And large it was. It was the size of a mandolin. A bolt of remorse creased his palate. Sixty years of canny scuttling had ended on the plate of a man unsure of his own name.

Nevertheless, Quick laid waste to the poor creature, interrupted several times by acquaintances welcoming him back. Ginger would lean in and prompt him: Sam Perkins, Erich van Haldenburg, Henka Lupin, Judd Marney.

Then came a face he recognized immediately. His sworn and bitter enemy, Edwin Plopp. Inside his belly the lobster twitched.

Plopp, a producer, had taken Quick's screenplay, *Sinners All,* a Shakespearean-quality tragedy, and had butchered it, absolutely obliterated it. Quick's painstakingly drawn diabolical antagonist, a supranatural creature never actually seen on film, had been changed into an evil baby. An evil baby floating in a magic birdcage, squinting evilly at passersby.

The withering scorn that greeted the evil baby only equaled the withering scorn heaped on the screenplay – of which Edwin Plopp's illiterate minions had changed Quick's every last word. But had left his name. Quick's fragile, fledgling career had been grotesquely mangled.

He limped forward, unable to fly, his agent and lawyer deserting him at the next corner. Next thing he knew he was in residence at Grigson Putty, an enclosure completion technician.

Acid-tongued revenge sitting coldly on his tongue, but his assault on Plopp was halted by Ginger's whisper, "This is Michael Dotson."

Michael Dotson was entirely pleasant and had wished him well.

Quick had shaken the producer's hand, lost and bewildered. Was this related to the new people at Grigson and his apartment which wasn't his?

More of the utterly unexplainable. He poked his thigh with a silver fork. It hurt. This wasn't a dream.

It was too big to think about.

Postprandial coffee arrived.

This was the moment Ginger had been waiting for. She would have to ask because Linden would obviously never get around to it. "Linden," she began, "I've kept my promise up to now. But now it's killing me and I really have to know."

Quick had grown afraid of moments like these. Who knew what he had promised? And to whom? Under what duress? "What was the promise and to whom was it directed?"

"It was to Dr. Boother."

"So ask him."

"I can't."

"Why not?"

"It's about you."

"Well, what is it?"

"I want to know about Temple Topper."

Predictably, Quick drew a blank. "Uhh, who is Temple Topper?"

"Tanya Topper's first cousin."

Quick judged himself no better informed. "Okay. And?"

Ginger's disappointment was visible. "Ohhhh. Dr. Boother was right."

Quick tamped down a flare of anger. "Look. I'm getting a little sick of Dr. Boother's behind-the-back pronouncements. Why don't you tell me plainly what's on your mind?"

"Tanya Topper is the sister of Tipper."

"Tipper Topper."

"Exactly. Now do you remember?"

Quick was getting seriously annoyed. "I guess I don't remember anything. Who are these vermin?"

"They're not vermin, they're Americans. You're so

prejudiced. They're the anesthesiologists."

"*Anesthesiologists?"*

"A family of anesthesiologists."

"But who the fuck are they, Ginger? I've never heard of them."

"Oh, yes you have. They're your people."

"*My* people??"

Ginger smiled a little smile at other diners, now spectators. For a split second she entertained the thought that this was *not* Linden Thackeray. "They're your characters, Linden. In the movie you won your Academy Award for."

"Ohhhh." Things were not clear but at least they were translucent.

"Is it coming back to you now? Tipper is the lead character in *Bubbles.*"

"Tipper Tucker."

"Topper."

"Topper Tucker." Quick was still murky.

"*No.* Tipper Tocker. *Damn it.* I mean Tipper Topper."

"For chrissakes, Ginger, get to the point. Please."

Ginger's eyes were full. "Before your accident, back when you were in a good mood, you promised me you'd write me a part in Bubbles III."

All became clear. But before he could think of the appropriate reply, he became aware that Ginger was staring at something over his shoulder. "Oh, *great,*" she spat.

"Great what?"

"One of your exes just came in. I'm going to the ladies room." She flounced off in high style.

So this was fame. The focus of every eye, the cause of every idle fork, stopped in its progress so its utenser might listen. Quick felt a thick redness rush to his head.

It took a physical effort to raise his eyes from the tablecloth. There was the breadbasket. With the red linen napkin. Draped carelessly over crumbs.

Suddenly a woman in a little black dress walked past his shoulder and turned to him. Tall and willowy, yet full-breasted, dramatic fall of chestnut brown hair framed a perfect face: sculpted, arched eyebrows over green eyes, full lips, an upturned little nose, flawless milk skin punctuated with a few dark freckles. Her sheer beauty commanded the eye to stare, perhaps to see.

Quick felt drunk. The woman sat down beside him, looking into his eyes, and unknowingly, into his parched and tiny soul. Quick was incapable of speech. Women of this caliber were beyond fantasy. A perfectly manicured hand was laid softly on his forearm, the forearm so recently of Grigson Putty and the roach coach. In a voice of languid, liquid velvet, the apparition inquired of his health. "Heard you've been ill, Linny. How are we really?"

Quick spread his hands helplessly. Words were rafts, flimsy and out of reach in a swift current. "Uh, uh, I'm fit as a furdle, I mean fiddle," he managed, barely. He watched her breathe and the swell of her breasts against the shiny black silk pulverized what remained of his mind. He tried in vain to look elsewhere, anywhere.

"You always did like my tits, Linny," she said, "as well you should."

"I, uh, should?"

"Of course you should. You bought and paid for them. Two sets, actually."

His mind was processing information slowly. Where were the other ones?

"I guess it's true," said the angel.

His hamster-wheel upstairs started moving again. "What's true? Don't make dangerous assumptions."

She examined him. "They say your dive from the sign gave you some sort of freaky amnesia. That you don't really know who you are."

"As usual in this town, bullshit is the coin of the realm."

"Of course it is, Linny. Do you remember our daughter's name?

Daughter? Hadn't heard of her. No pictures round the house. "Of course I know her name. Let's not play stupid games."

Alison cocked her head. "It's true, then. Jesus."

"I assure you," Quick stated coldly, "that I'm in full control of my faculties and resent implications to the contrary."

Beauty just shook her head. "We've never had a daughter, Linny. I'd've lost my figure. My name is Alison, by the way." She rose, reached into her bosom, pulled out a business card. "Meet my new myrmidon-at-law. Call him." She looked around. "We have a lot to talk about. I'm tired of dumps like this."

Then the dream turned on her heel and walked into the night. Quick looked at the card she had given him.

John Webster Fennis
Attorney-at-Law

Chapter 20

Throw the Doc a Bone

Dr. Boother massaged his temples. Babysitting was hard work. Especially with a forty-one-year-old baby rich as Croesus. Rich as Gates, an allusion surely making its way down the pike, had not yet settled comfortably on his tongue. He watched infant Thackeray clamber out of the pool. What did Ginger see in him? Thackeray fell into the wicker chair beside Dr. Boother, shaking his head like a wet dog. Boother felt the droplets on his skin, ignored them. If only Thackeray didn't pay so incredibly well. "So, Linden, how are we this morning?"

Quick stretched luxuriously. A few laps in the morning every day? You couldn't beat it. He felt stronger, quicker, sharper.

"How are we this morning, Linden?" repeated Boother, exercising professional calm.

Quick stretched again. "We's kickin' ass, doc, kickin' ass." He downed a large glass of fresh-squeezed OJ, looked into the clear, blue water.

He had really come to really appreciate the Mexican tiling around the inside lip of the pool. It was classy. Sick and rich was one thing. Sick and working poor, à la Grigson Putty, was another.

He searched Dr. Boother's face. Perhaps he'd toss the doc a bone. The doc looked needy. After all, from the vantage point of money, a doctor was just another employee, eager to please.

"I think," Quick paused as if thinking, "I think I'm more, how would you say it, in touch with my feelings."

Whatever that meant. Feelings, schmeelings. He watched Boother perk up. Like water on a pansy.

"This is good news, Linden," said Boother, "very good news." Feelings were emotional markers associated with facts. And facts were the building blocks of memory. And memory was the backbone of life. Which heralded his eventual unemployment. Obviously, it would be best to take things slowly.

Boother gained his feet, started pacing. "What you've suffered, Linden, is what I call an elliptical psychocentric dislocative episode. Basically, your mind is out of round."

Quick nodded. His mind, as far as he knew, had never been *in round*. That was why life seldom rolled in an unvarying direction. Maybe Boother-quack would pull some flashcards out of his ass. Yet, since he, Quick, was apparently stuck in this life, he might as well get on with it. "What are my chances, doc?"

"Good," said Boother, "given time and motivation in the trajectory of recovery and reconstruction."

"Hmmm," said Quick, recognizing the tenor of paycheck-padding when he heard it.

"What I recommend, Linden," continued Boother, "is returning to work, rubbing elbows with your colleagues. Getting your mind off the immediate situation. What do you think?"

Quick poured himself another glass of OJ, drank deeply, savored the sunshine warming his feet. He'd heard about Thackeray Entertainment. From Stamler. And he'd done a little research online. So be it. It was time. Other than gravediggers, he was possessed of an unusual opportunity. It was time to start at the top.

Chapter 21

Thackeray Entertainment

Quick looked at himself in the mirror. He, or his alter-ego, Thackeray, possessed fifty suits. Quick had owned but one, a gray sharkskin escapee from a thrift store on La Brea. Aged but stylish, and just one size smallish, a choking spasm up the street at Pink's Hot Dogs had split both pants and jacket and provided street theater for the four score gawking in line.

But the Armani fitted him perfectly, the tips of folded fingers meeting sleeve's edge at the heel of his hand. His belt, from Bergdorf-Goodman, was neither parsimonious nor overly generous. A silk Beatles tie, patterned after Abbey Road, set off a crisp white shirt. Cole Haan shoes gently spread the palm of his foot.

A sixty-foot steel-grey Cadillac limousine burbled in the brick driveway downstairs. Waiting to whisk him off to a company bearing *his* name. Which employed one hundred and sixty people. Quick stared into his own eyes. Who the hell was this man?

He'd requested his fingerprints be taken again. Boother had shrugged and complied. The fingerprints were those of Linden Paul Thackeray. "Take the Sherlock Holmes approach," counseled Boother. "Eliminate the impossible. Then embrace what's left. However improbable it may be."

Quick nodded, that day sick with doubt. Wild and crazy, assuredly so. Just plain crazy? No. No. Never. How was it possible? His name was Michael James Quick. It just had to be. He'd had a life.

Ginger appeared beside him in an expensive eddy of perfume. "Don't we look handsome today," she purred with a smile, unnecessarily straightening his tie.

Oh, God, not now, he thought. But here it came, and here it was, that tug at his belt. What had begun as a startling realization of fantasy had changed into the gray tyranny of the commonplace. Not joyless, certainly. Oh, well. Ginger was part snake charmer, part sword-swallower, and had channeled aspects of young Demosthenes. As always, he warmed to her task.

Sixty seconds later he was robbed of all strength. Opening his eyes, he remembered the limousine downstairs. "Come back soon," said Ginger, naughtily. Quick nodded. If only she'd fall for Dr. Boother.

The limousine swept through west L.A., turning on Pico, passing Quick's favorite golf course.

Not that he'd ever been there. It was the concept of Hillcrest that made him feel triumphant. Human. Brave.

Quick didn't play golf. In concert with Samuel Clemens, he considered it a good walk ruined. It was the historical significance of this particular expanse of green that delighted him.

Hillcrest had been built in response to Jewish exclusion from the Los Angeles Country Club. Jews were not allowed even as guests. A proud time for America. The Jews were left to build a course of their own. So they did. On the first hole they struck oil.

Now this was a god you could get behind. Quick smiled. He himself had wanted to be Jewish. For three weeks. He had read Michener's *The Source*. He had been profoundly affected. At a shapeless time in early adulthood, he felt drawn to a society of strict rule and boundary under the eye of a jealous god. But he had not acted and gradually the feeling evaporated, synapse by synapse, leaving him, once again, without counsel or philosophy, another rootless, skeptical, lapsed Catholic.

The limousine was waved on to the Imperial lot by a sad-faced security muffin. Probably another writer. After passing Old New York and a few sharp turns this way and that, there it was. Thackeray Entertainment.

Thackeray Entertainment.

Three stories of green-tinted glass and white concrete. Shaded by a graceful, transplanted grove of aspen. Christ, thought Quick, *wow*. Did I really build this place? *Me?*

It was the kind of place, in his old life, where even the secretaries were too good for him. Smacking their gum, smiling up at him with zero interest, brusquely cutting off his conversational sorties to answer the phone. Billy Goldstone's office. Rupert Finn's office. John Campisi's office.

Never once had any of these long-legged women evinced a scrap of interest in the writer, the living artist underneath the thinning hair. An *artist*. A man whose ambition throbbed as the heartbeat of civilization. *No*. They were all too busy drinking apple martinis, dropping ecstasy, and being degraded by six-figure psychopaths in German automobiles.

The driver opened his door and Quick stepped into the afternoon sun. Almost immediately the green glass doors of Thackeray Entertainment flew back and a gaggle of well-dressed men and women tumbled out, waving excitedly. Quick resisted the urge to look behind him. These were his employees, most probably, and they were most probably waving at him. He waved and they waved some more. Now they encircled him with proffered handshakes and hearty backslaps. It was great to be home.

"Let me show you to your office, Mr. Thackeray," said a thin-faced young man in a well-cut Italian suit.

Quick could feel the young man's eyes. They were digging, probing, searching for the depths of Quick's infirmity. "It's great to have you back, Mr. Thackeray." The young man paused. "By the way, as you know," he continued, carefully, "I'm Orville Mayberry."

Quick had nodded, thinly, vacantly.

"Your personal assistant," added Mayberry.

"Ah, yes. Bayberry." Quick affected a grand manner. Mayberry was an employee. "You stand recalled, Bayberry. We've been talking on the phone."

Mayberry looked nothing like he sounded. On the phone he sounded like a respectful kid. In person he radiated ambition like a spider. "I think I speak for everyone, Mr. Thackeray, when I say that we're all chomping at the bit to really get going on Bubbles III."

Bubbles III? Jesus Christ. Even the pool guy had pestered him about it. Everyone wanted in, wanted a part, wanted a job. Bubbles I & II must have been good. Well, they had to be. Or Bubbles III wouldn't exist. Though only Ginger was truly focused on a daily basis. On a twenty-minute basis. Which was part of the problem.

Mayberry smiled. "Bubbles III is an important film. Essentially the capstone, so to speak."

Quick nodded. He was in a different universe. This proved it yet again. An avid filmgoer, certainly he would have heard of a Bubbles franchise of sizable dimension. Or this could be one of those contradictory universes. Where Pi was an even number. Where cubes had five sides and the mutually exclusionary marched shoulder to shoulder.

"By the way," Mayberry coughed to introduce a change of subject, "I'm in full communication with Dr. Boother."

"I see." Bastard Boother. Who knew what manure

he'd been spreading? "Are *you* fully in round, Mr. Mayberry?"

"Yes, sir. Tip top. A1. Ready to push Bubbles III down the runway and into the sky."

Quick nodded. Smooth bastard. Round bastard. And bullshit Boother had been blabbing behind his back.

Chapter 22

Forty-Five Minutes

Alone in his office, the fear returned. His only true friend in the world was Leslie Stewart. She seemed to be the only human being not interested in Bubbles III. The only one willing to believe in Michael Quick. "You don't want a part or something?" he had queried.

"Are you kidding? You couldn't pay me to be in on that."

"Actually, that's exactly what I could do."

"Well, I don't want to be paid for that."

"Why not?"

"Life is humiliating enough without getting associated with movies like that. Fart movies with messages. It's too much to bear. Thank you for asking. The answer is no."

Bubbles in the Tub must have been some picture, thought Quick. He'd have to get around to seeing it. Like Stravinsky's *Rite of Spring*. Dividing the people. It was funny and comforting that Leslie drew a distinction between him and his work. He would keep Stravinsky in mind.

His relationship with Leslie had become slightly difficult. Maybe not difficult, *labored* might be a better word. Choosing women in his old life was simply a matter of accepting or rejecting the candidates from the extremely shallow pool desperate enough to consider him. If they met his compromised threshold of attractiveness, he had rarely summoned the strength to walk away.

Very quickly he admired their intelligence, and once he admired their intelligence, he was willing to lend them any and all qualities they might need. To rip his heart out. But things were different now. All the women were well above his threshold. How was he to judge?

Leslie was looking at him. "What's wrong with you?"

"What are you talking about?"

"That look on your face."

"What look?"

Quick used to think he was in control of his face. But he wasn't. Regardless of intention, his face broadcast the truth. He was probably sending out confusion, irresolution. It made perfect sense. His standards were askew. He liked Leslie very much. Very, very much. Sometimes he wanted to kiss her again and sometimes he felt she harbored the same idea. But she was his only true friend in the current universe. What would happen if he made a move, was accepted, and then was bowled over by another Ginger with size 38D brains? He would preserve his relationship with Leslie as it currently existed. He would move ahead, perhaps, when signals were unambiguous.

He looked around. Where the hell was everybody?

Bayberry stuck his head in.

Chapter 23

Slow Learner

"We were looking everywhere for you, sir," said Mayberry.

Quick had confounded everyone by hiding in the guest lounge. It had looked like a fucking office, for godsake. *His* office, he'd guessed. He'd been waiting in there for forty-five minutes. Like an imbecile.

Mayberry showed him to his office suite on the fourth floor. It was cavernous. Two beautiful women were waiting for him. Mayberry bowed, smiled, departed. The tall, leggy blonde introduced herself as Anne. "Anne Bullard, as I'm sure you remember, Mr. Thackeray. Welcome back."

"Hello, Anne," said Quick. Anne was slim, trim, mid-thirties. Anne introduced the second woman. "And this is Stacy Green," there was a pause, "as I'm sure you remember."

Stacy Green had green eyes and dark hair. She was younger than her colleague and very, very pretty in a sharp-featured sort of way. How had he ever managed to get any work done?

"Welcome back, Mr. Thackeray," said Miss Green, in a velvety contralto. Leslie flickered and dimmed in his mind. With effort, Quick set her back on her pedestal.

Quick nodded. "Thank you very much, both of you. How nice to see both of you again." It was quite amazing actually, the women he'd forgotten. "You've heard of my little problem," he continued, acknowledging their concern, "and I ask, in advance, that you forgive me if I seem to be both coming and going."

The women were entirely sympathetic. "Well, sir," said Anne,"we'll always be here for you."

"When you get back," added Stacy.

They all laughed.

After a while they stopped. Quick looked around, he wasn't sure where to sit exactly. Maybe he had just laid out on the couch, ate grapes, gave orders. Anne sensed his predicament. She pointed to a wide door. "That's your private office in there."

"Of course," said Quick.

There was a plaque on the door. It contained three reviews of *Bubbles in the Tub.*

FILM
New U.S. release: Bubbles in the Tub
By Howard Densmore

Every once in while a film come along so perfectly aligned with the times, so truly expressing the zeitgeist, it's like watching Babe Ruth calling and hitting a five-hundred-foot home run to centerfield. Bubbles in the Tub, written and directed by Linden Thackeray, produced by Charles Finkster, is one of those films. It's a home run.

FILM
New U.S. release: Bubbles in the Tub
By Dan Cartwright

A five-star, laugh-aloud lowbrow comedy about slipping, sliding, and outrageous flatulence, this Imperial production expertly juxtaposes and intercuts scenes depicting the shameful truth of third-world juvenile starvation. Bubbles in the Tub makes us laugh and cry at the same time.

FILM

Worldwide release: Bubbles in the Tub

By Tom Pike

The beautifully drawn characters of Ed and Tipper Whigson invite us into their world of plenty only to reveal their pain, high emptiness, and chagrin. Yet, as ineluctable as an alimentary bubble floating to the surface to gently explode in sulfurous reprimand, we come to ask ourselves how different are the dreams of third-world youngsters? Where is their hope for happiness and justice as their futures are sold and resold in the redolent marketplace of avarice and greed? Go see Bubbles in the Tub.

Wow. And Leslie had called it a fart movie. He opened the door and regarded his office.

It was as big as a game preserve.

It had several tall trees, a rusty steel giraffe and a reflecting pool. A huge window looked over the lot. His desk was a vast mahogany plane the size of a one-bedroom apartment.

There was nothing on it except for one thing. There, toward a corner of the plane, resplendent in its solitary magnificence, gleaming goldly, was the Holy Grail of Hollywood, an Oscar. Quick involuntarily gasped. Then walked slowly around the desk, toward the supreme accolade.

He half-expected it to retreat from his grasp but it didn't. Maybe it had been his labors rewarded. Best Original Screenplay—*Bubbles in the Tub*—Linden Thackeray. And Leslie, high on her horse, had called it a fart movie. Fart movies didn't win Oscars.

The statue itself was impressive. It was heavy and the golden luster seemed to seep into his soul. Oscar stood tall, proud, and stoic. He's seen a lot before tasting victory. He'd shrugged off indifference and contempt. He had walked resolutely through the fires of skepticism and ridicule to drink the sweet waters of vindication. And then, from his lofty position, so well deserved, he had been humble, gracious, and generous.

It was then that he heard a long, plangent sigh. He spun, startled. Across the room, someone raised herself up from a white leather couch. Nature's gifts, augmented by the surgeon's art, were displayed to maximum advantage. Long fingers pushed back a tress of platinum blonde hair. "You act like you've never seen an Oscar before, Linden."

Michael tried to keep his eyes from her gravity-defying breasts. "Uh, uh, I ..."

"Or is it that you don't remember me, Linden? Or us?"

"Us?" Quick was staggered. Maybe he really was the schlub Michael Quick. Only a god of infinite cruelty would erase a memory like this. This was a sign, surely. He should've jumped ship for the God of Hole Number One.

Blondie got to her feet. She had been fashioned carefully by angels. "I'm Alana," said the dream. "Alana Maxwell. You don't remember a thing, do you?"

There was no use pretending. "No," he said wretchedly.

"You poor thing."

Quick put hand to forehead. "Am I."

Alana sat back down on the couch, patted the space beside her.

"Come sit with me, Linden," she said.

"Okay," said Quick.

Slowly the dream leaned into him, and before he had a chance to summon his intelligence, her lips had touched his own and he was lost. Finally she broke away.

"I think you're getting the idea," said Alana.

"I'm a fast learner," he replied. He reached for her and she melted into his arms. He would delay his rapprochement with the Jealous God. Then the phone rang. He tried to ignore it but it kept ringing. It was a restricted line but, Christ Jesus, it could be anyone. He didn't have time for anyone. He detached himself from heaven, hurried to the desk, picked up the phone. "Linden Thackeray." It was the first time he'd used the name officially.

It was Anne Bullard. "Excuse me, Mr. Thackeray. John Webster Fennis is on line three."

Who the fuck was John Webster Fennis? Then he remembered.

Fennis was the reptile Alison had retained. "Miss Bullard," said Quick, with force, "fuck John Webster Fennis."

"Yes, sir." The line went dead. Quick headed back to the couch.

"Where's the remote?" inquired Alana, tucking various things in.

"You want to *watch TV*?" Quick was angered, chagrined, and amazed.

Alana was on her feet. "I forgot. You don't know anything." She walked to his desk, looked around. On the bookcase behind his desk she spied what she was looking for.

"Why do you need—"

Alana aimed the remote in the vicinity of the screening area, clicked. Immediately the window overlooking the lot darkened, the bookcase of famous scripts revolved to reveal a wet bar, and the interoffice deadbolt slammed home.

Alana smiled. "Let's take a trip down memory lane, Linden."

He could get used to this, "I'm ready for a trip."

Alana led him back to the couch. "Where were we?" asked Quick. Within seconds, like addicts, they had taken up where they had left off.

She broke away again. "What now?" asked Quick of the angel.

Panting, she raised a finger. "Just one thing."

"Name it," replied Quick.

"We have to talk."

"Talk? *Now*? About what?"

"About us."

"About us?"

"About us and Bubbles III."

"A-ha." Everything became clear. Alana Maxwell was not all that different from the pool guy. Then he felt a tug at his belt. Though the differences were significant. Minutes later, he was robbed of all strength.

Chapter 24

Grooving with the Arhats

There was Alana Maxwell. There was Kitty Marcus. There was Tracy Cox. There was Alicia Stewart. There was Mazy Starr, aka Marsha Leibman-Whitney. There was Latournishia Roberts. And there, in the background, like a crocodile, was the insatiable Ginger. So it was no real surprise that he missed Leslie's chess tournament. One day, despite his thousand assurances, the tournament was in the past. *Shit.* He called and called and called but nothing. She wouldn't return. He could hardly blame her.

Meanwhile, various aspects of Bubbles III went forward as planned. Secretly he began to fear it. How would he honor his promises to seventeen leading ladies? Unless he could make Bubbles III into an aquatic extravaganza. Maybe the ladies might be cast as water lilies or something. That was an idea. Esther Williams. That was the name.

And that wouldn't work anyway. They didn't make pools that big anymore. And some of them probably couldn't swim. But, uh, they probably could float.

His phone rang. Anne Bullard. "Yes," he said, trying to sound busy.

"You have a visitor, Mr. Thackeray."

"Who?"

"Miss Candy Lee Jopsie."

Of course, he'd never heard of Candy Lee Jopsie. But he knew what she wanted. "Tell Miss Jopsie to go away, I'm busy," he said. Though moral fiber had worn thin, still a few filaments remained.

"I'll see you tonight, Mr. Thackeray," said Anne Bullard, a twinkle in her voice. "I can't wait, Miss Bullard."

Tonight was the night.

Now Quick and a thousand of his new friends exited the Chinese Theater. Quick walked down the red carpeted walkway, velvet ropes on each side. Thousands cheered him, the empty vessel. He waved and they roared. He waved again and they roared again. He looked back at the marquee. There they were. *Bubbles in the Tub,* and *Bubble Trouble.* It was a re-premier. Like re-losing one's virginity.

He was shaken. The two movies were some of the worst movies he'd ever seen in his whole life. Leslie had been exactly right. They were fart movies stinking with messages. With *Tub* it had been the pitiful plight of third-world children. With *Trouble,* it had been global warming. Yet he, author of *The Eagle and the Dove,* spiritual contemporary of Shakespeare, had created them. It was a different universe. It had to be.

Not that farts weren't funny. In their place. A gentle reminder of common humanity. You farted and so did the Pope. If detected, the shrug would be the same. It wasn't the farts. It was the heavy helping of pious message mixed in with them. It was pandering, that was the word. I pander. You pander. He panders. It was soul-pandering. How could he ever look anyone in the eye ever again?

Nevertheless, pen and paper were thrust in his face and he signed and signed and signed. Finally Ginger grabbed his arm and lead him to the very long Hummer limousine. There was a crush at the window and then the vehicle broke away. Ginger gave a shake of her head. "That little bimbo in red was out of line if you ask me."

"Who's asking?" said Quick. He had come to enjoy

thwarting Ginger's little affirmations. And, by the way, what bimbo had he missed?

"You saw her. You were looking."

"What are you talking about?"

"The girl who wasn't wearing underwear, Linden. Jesus."

"I didn't notice, actually."

"Everyone else did." Ginger folded her arms under her bounteous rack.

Quick sought to mollify her. He liked Ginger. She was amiable and undemanding with one fatal appetite. "Don't worry about her. She's probably just a girl from Ball'o Yarn, Oklahoma who got a little too excited."

"What a butthead, Linden." Ginger seemed hurt.

Quick had no idea why she was upset. "Did I say something that upset you?"

"Yes."

"What? What did I say?"

"You know what you said."

Though Quick was unsure of where he stood, he knew this particular innocence was not worth defending. He threw up his hands.

"I'm from Ball o' Yarn, Linden." Ginger turned to stare anywhere but in his direction.

"Sorry. That was just an expression."

"Sometimes I wonder about you, Linden."

Ten minutes later the limousine pulled up in front of Tinseltown's hottest spot, Club Lust. He was inundated by well-wishers offering congratulations and angling for employment. He was offered cocaine, heroin, marijuana, ecstasy, and oral and anal sex. He settled for French fries, a Heineken and a booth in the back. He watched, goggle-eyed, at the diversions of the rich.

The amount of illegality consummated in plain sight was utterly beyond his comprehension. Where were the police? Where were they? Did they not know about this address? Here in the middle of Sunset Strip?

Bribery was a function of human nature, true. But, as Michael Quick, he had never witnessed it, nor had it been a tool in hand. You needed money. Bribery, apparently, worked like nothing else. Giving in to a mere fraction of the temptations would be the equivalent of taking a chisel to his liver.

But time eroded his will and he succumbed to five or six of the offerings. He had never been in the company of so many funny, fascinating people.

The party continued at Jean Harlow's former residence in Whitley Heights, high above a seedy section of Hollywood. A chorus line of salaamers welcomed him with cries of *Bubbles in the Tub, Bubbles in the Tub!* He was immediately led to the secret room where further bottled gods and powder princes held sway. Emerging, he found the living room had been cleared for dancing and that Ginger was eager to dance with her prize, Linden Thackeray.

He attempted to dance and briefly found himself weightless and delighted. But then vectors of gravity seized him and he began moving steadily and irresistibly to his left. Soon he was dancing by himself and then he was in the kitchen.

Where an orgy was in progress. Stupefied, he stared eyes wide at the acrobats. One of the bangers separated from a bangee and turned to him. "Hey, buddy," said the furry man with a gold medallion, "pass the butter."

Butter? It took concepts appreciable time to sink through his sodden cerebellum. Butter. Was that *Apocalypse Now* or *Last Tango in Paris*? Then the bangee looked up over her shoulder from the butcher-block table. "Hey, I know you," she said, pants around her ankles.

"You do?"

"Yes," she said brightly, "I'm Candy Lee Jopsie."

He'd heard that name somewhere.

"Hey, buddy. The butter." Gold medallion was getting impatient. But it was all too much for Quick. He spied the kitchen door and made for it.

Suddenly he was in in the garden and all was silent and peaceful. The lights of Los Angeles twinkled softly below him and honeysuckle wafted in on the breeze. Butter was bad for the heart. Ahead was a gazebo. It was probably full of spiders. He took a deep breath and slowly the two moons resolved into one.

Abruptly, through the haze, he realized he was horribly lonely. Leslie. Leslie. Leslie. Leslie. He heard shrieks of laughter and breaking glass.

He didn't want to think about who might be doing what to whom. He felt a tiny pinch in the inner corner of his eye. Good god, was he about to break off a tear? The four states of inebriation: the jocose, the bellicose, the lachrymose, the comatose. He must be in the third state. Which meant he'd probably been a spectacle earlier. Leslie. If only he'd gone to the tournament.

A breeze gusted. He closed his eyes. This would be the perfect time for a vision. An epiphanic and clarifying bolt of inspiration. Like Indians on mountaintops. Life-changing and profound. A spirit on the wind. Universal, yet personal. Then he heard a voice.

"Linden." The voice was an unhurried whisper. Timeless and clear. "Linden."

"Yes, spirit, speak to me," he replied mentally.

"Linden," said the voice.

"Speak to me," he continued in silence.

"Linden."

Maybe the spirits were mentally deaf. Or probably he was sending on the wrong mental frequency. What did he know about interstellar communications anyway?

"Linden." The voice was urgent now.

"It is I," he responded aloud, with full sonority. "Speak."

"Linden. Jesus Christ. You must really be shit-faced."

Grooving with the arhats died in the moment. He turned angrily—to face one of the most beautiful women he'd ever seen. He checked first with one eye, then the other. His ire evaporated like a mist on the Mojave. "Can I help you?"

The woman sat down beside him, looked into his face. "You don't know me, do you?"

Another tragedy. Quick shook his head slowly. Face, body, hands. All exquisite. "If only I did," he stated, honestly.

"I've heard you weren't well."

Quick tapped his temple. "Only up here." Where it didn't seem to matter all that much.

The woman leaned to kiss him softly on the cheek. "You were my husband, Linny."

A thick glob of self-pity plopped into his mind. He looked into the green, green eyes framed by red, red hair. "Help me, uh ..." He ended on a mournful inflection of humbled hope.

Beauty tapped her chest between the swelling monuments of Dr. Heisenberg, plastic surgeon. "I'm Carla," she said, each syllable a pearl.

Quick shook his head, then looked deep into her eyes. "Help me, Carla." *Help me, Carla, help, help me, Carla* sang the Beach Boys in his mind.

Carla's eyes glistened. Sweet Christ in Jerusalem, thought Quick, she's crying. And before he could truly savor the thought they were locked in a deep sensuous kiss. Then he felt a tug at his belt.

Later, robbed doubly of all strength, he wandered

back into the shindig, grabbed a Diet Coke. Ginger appeared. She seemed a little miffed. "Where've you been? I've been looking all over for you."

"I dunno. Around, I guess."

Ginger looked him up and down. "You look like you've been gardening. You're filthy."

Quick examined himself. The knees of his trousers were black with ground-in dirt. "Uh," he theorized, "they, uh, play croquet out there."

"Croquet? In the dark?"

"It's more challenging. And the moon is out."

Ginger looked into his face, suspicious. "You must have been playing with a short wood."

Quick nodded probatively. "And it was a difficult angle." It had been. He wondered what Carla's clothes might look like.

Then Carla walked by. Looking as perfect as she had upon first sight. "Hi, Linny," she said with all innocence. She tucked a business card into his jacket pocket. "You'll be needing this." Off she walked.

Ginger stared daggers at her back. "You've been talking to her?"

"She seemed friendly."

"You said, after your last screwing, that you'd never talk to her again."

"I said that?"

"You certainly did. You swore it. And, boy, did you get screwed."

Better check that card, thought Quick. He pulled it out of his pocket.

John Webster Fennis
Attorney-at-Law

Chapter 25

A New Plan

Fennis was running a straight flush. He now represented all the women Quick had supposedly married. All of them wanted the same thing, and Fennis, the humanitarian, was there to help them get it.

Maybe attorneys became inured to it, or perhaps they had a natural tolerance to venom. The average citizen was sickened and frightened by coldly worded legal missives. Demanding this, demanding that, summoning him forthwith. John Webster Fennis needed killing.

Five ex-wives; that was a lot of love gone bad. What could he possibly have done? If he had indeed done anything. He had read somewhere the sad fact the most men do not marry the woman they loved the most. Well, he had tried, apparently. Certainly the man who married five times could honestly be called an optimist.

The phone on his desk rang the interior ring. He'd been feeling depressed since the re-premier party. He'd seen Candy Lee Jopsie in action. Maybe she was calling now. He picked up the phone. "Yes?"

It was Anne Bullard. "You have a call on line three. Leslie Stewart." His heart leapt in his chest. He thought he had lost her.

"Put her through." Forty minutes later they sat across from one another at Kate Mantilini's. She looked at him sternly. He brought fist to heart three times. "Mea culpa, mea culpa, mea maxima culpa."

Leslie's expression did not change and he feared the

worst. Then she smiled and sunshine flooded his world. "I'm so glad to see you," he gushed. "I thought – "

"You thought what?"

"I know I missed the tournament. And then you didn't return my calls. I thought you were done with me."

"You're a butthead, Michael." She took a bite of the excellent French bread and he swam in the seas of perfect happiness. "You're cutting quite a swath with this Thackeray business," she continued. "The re-premier at the Chinese Theater and all."

Some might call it a swath. His liver had judged it an assault. "A swath? What are you talking about?"

"You're in all the papers. And they say you're in the running for an Oscar with *Bubble Trouble.*"

"I despise *Bubble Trouble.*"

"It deserved to be despised." She took another bite of bread. "I was at the Chinese the other night."

"You were?"

"You didn't see me wave?"

"No. I'm sorry."

"I had my special red dress on. I thought you might invite me to the after party."

In other words a bullet had parted his hair. "The afterparty? The definition of a bore. I wouldn't force that on anyone."

"You have a very pretty girlfriend."

"Don't be too liberal with titles. She's more like my keeper. She knows all the people I'm supposed to know. She came with the package."

"Nice package."

"Don't worry."

"That must be Ginger."

"Yes. Don't worry."

"Why should I worry? You're not beholden to me."

Quick recognized infirm footing. He made line for solid ground. "I read in the paper about your tournament."

Leslie smiled widely. "You're talking to the new county champion."

Quick was sincerely delighted. "Congratulations. There're twelve million people in L.A. County. That's a major accomplishment."

Leslie was very pleased. "Thank you, Michael," she said, basking. "I am very proud." She paused a second. "Are you getting in over your head? You know. With this Thackeray business?"

"Of course not," he began, but then the truth was on the tip of his tongue and out it came. "Way over my head." From which he quickly backtracked, "I'm in control, but, you know, the water's fast and things distract me."

"What kinds of things?"

Quick tried to quickly move his mind past the ilk of Candy Lee Jopsie. It would be disaster if his low predilections were legible on his face. "Details of Bubbles III. Preproduction hassles. Stuff like that." He attempted to present boredom and irritation.

Leslie seemed to accept it. He had cleverly mixed fact and fiction. "So how much did you despise your movies at the Chinese?"

"You want to see some self-flagellation. It's probably unhealthy." He shrugged. "But I guess I could live without that part of my legacy."

"Of course you could. They're shameless, sexist, piggish, and juvenile."

"That's why they made money."

"Adding to the sedimentary layer of crap under our cultural foundations."

Even though he agreed with her, a strange loyalty

had risen within him. "Something has to be under the foundations. Or the foundations would be floating in mid-air."

"Then they wouldn't be foundations."

"Exactly."

They glared at one another. Then broke into laughter. She smiled enchantingly. "You're Linden Thackeray now. You sneeze and realign the borders of nations. You say Bubbles III and girls drop their pants."

Had he given himself away? "What's your point?"

"My point is you have the power. Why don't you use it? Why don't you make some movies that count?"

Not a bad idea. Not a bad idea at all. *Good* idea. He nodded as if acknowledging her apprehension of the obvious. "What makes you think that wasn't my plan all along?"

"Because you're not that smart," she replied.

She was right. They both laughed again.

Chapter 26

The Eagle and the Dove

Revolutionary thoughts once thunk could not be unthunk. What movie would Linden Thackeray like to bring to the world? How about a movie by his alter-ego, Michael Quick?

How about Quick's battered and scorned masterpiece, *The Eagle and the Dove?*

Though the script did not exist in the new reality, Quick remembered the gist of it. And what did that say about the new reality? Never mind. He was going day by day now. He would and could literally rewrite the script.

Quick reached a toe past the Mexican tiling and dipped it into the pool. No time for swimming today. He sipped his orange juice. Yes, he could and would rewrite the script.

Dr. Boother had been most encouraged by his progress. "I'm most encouraged by your progress, Linden," said the doctor.

"I get a clean bill of health, you're saying?"

"The signposts point to optimism," Boother said cautiously, thinking of the little Jaguar coupe he had seen on Van Nuys Boulevard. "But we mustn't rush Mother Nature. Science is repeatability. We need consistent observations over a period of months."

Just another common payroll lamprey, thought Quick. "I'm thinkin' probably six to nine months, doc," he added, watching Boother's eyes register opportunity." Maybe longer."

"We can't be too careful, Linden, you're right."

Boother stroked his chin. Why settle for a Jaguar? What about a Porsche? And only yesterday had Ginger, for the first time, unambiguously touched his leg.

"Am I getting round, do you think?" pressed Quick.

Boother nodded judiciously. "Rounder. But not yet a sphere."

Quick took the news calmly, cleared his throat. "Well, doc, I better get back to work. Things are humming at the studio."

Boother rose to his feet. "That would be my recommendation, Linden." The doctor took five steps toward the house when he paused, turned back.

"Yes?" said Quick.

"Don't over-do things. Walk before you run."

Quick nodded. No doubt about it. A payroll lamprey.

◆ ◆ ◆

Later, from his office, Quick dialed up Charlie Finkster, president of Imperial Studios. Linden Thackeray was put right through.

Lunch that afternoon was in Finkster's private dining room at 1:42 pm. "You might be wondering about one-forty-two, Linden," said Finkster.

Quick hadn't given it a thought. "One-forty-two is the perfect time for me, personally, to achieve afternoon sustenance," said Finkster, spearing a stalk of braised asparagus.

Quick wondered if he should be interested.

"My dietician, Mrs. Undafelmi, is also a numerologist," continued the president of Imperial Studios. "I'll give you her number. She's a magician."

"Please," said Quick. Was Mrs. Undafelmi a magician as well, or merely a magician in the culinary/numerical interface environment?

After the eggless omelet with nonfat goat cheese and capers. Finkster set aside his fork. "So. Linden. I'm glad you're back at work. How goes Bubbles III?"

"Everyone at Thackeray Entertainment is rabid."

"You are less rabid."

"Yes."

"More omelet?"

"No, thank you."

"What are your reservations, Linden?"

"I don't think we should oversaturate the market. Two Bubbles appear sufficient. Three? I'm not sure."

"I'm not sure abandoning III in midstream is a good idea."

"It's hardly in midstream," Quick replied. "In fact, we're not even in the water. We know what it's going to be about—"

"Farts," interjected Finkster.

"—but the script is hardly begun."

"Farts are my favorite."

"It's actually in the pre-word stage, Charlie."

"It hardly needs words."

"Another of my objections."

"You don't want to write it."

"No." The truth was on the table.

"In a small way, Linden, I can hardly blame you. But this is a detail. There're fifty-thousand writers in this town. Forty-nine thousand nine hundred and ninety-nine of them would push their grandmothers down the stairs into a briar patch filled with amphetamine-injected rattlesnakes for the opportunity to write just the first draft."

Where was Finkster going here?

"Where I'm going, Linden, is you don't have to write it. We'll get it ghosted. And ghost-directed. You'll still get your fees and everything. It's perfect."

For the first time, in that instant, Quick recalled his efforts at Grigson Putty with rueful fondness. Recompensed however poorly, it was honest work. And though he complained bitterly about his plight, he toiled mightily and honorably to change his station. Albeit for naught.

Now he was world-famous for things he had not done and would be paid huge sums not to do more of them. A queasy, greasy wave rose within him. "I don't want anything to do with Bubbles III, Charlie. I don't want to write, I don't want to produce, I don't want to direct. I want to move on."

Finkster sipped his vitamin water and restrained his distress. Thackeray, although dumb as a post, was a franchise. He would have to be coddled until his senses returned. "What do you want to do?" inquired Finkster.

Quick sat back. He was a franchise. He had Finkster right where he wanted him. "What I want to do is a piece I call *The Eagle and Dove.*

Finkster repeated the title as if tasting it. "*The Eagle and the Dove.*" Apparently his judgment was mixed. "I like the first half, Linden, the Eagle. Sounds like action," he finished hopefully.

"It's not physical action," said Quick.

Finkster was confused. "Not physical action. What kind of action is it?"

"Metaphysical action."

"Metaphysical action?"

Quick could sense a confluence of minds. "It's about everything," gushed Quick. "Life, justice, love, temptation, regret."

Finkster set down his vitamin water. "There's a pretty narrow market for that everything stuff. What's the gist?"

"Imagine the Pope and Don Juan, the Yaqui

Indian," said Quick, but he trailed off on Finkster's blank look. "I'm talking about the Don Juan of the Carlos Casteneda books. Don Juan's a sorcerer, he's the nagual, the man of knowledge and power, he's the immortal Eagle."

"Immortal. Sorcery. I like that. How many divisions does the Pope have?" inquired Finkster, "confronting a sorcerer and all. I see drugs, spears, cauldrons, cannibals, that stuff?

Sprinkle in a few Nazis, maybe?"

"Exactly the opposite of that, Charlie. The Pope and Don Juan meet at a roadside diner on a lonely stretch of Highway 54 in New Mexico."

"And?"

"And what?"

"And what do they do?"

"What would the Pope and the Nagual do? They talk. They discuss the great issues of life. From soap scum to soul migration and everything in between.

"That covers a lot of ground."

"Immense ground."

"Is that all?" Finkster had given this ass every benefit of every doubt. What had happened to the man with the lowest common denominator of America so firmly in his grasp? Farts were huge.

"Is that *all?"* Quick repeated. Perhaps Finkster wasn't as smart as he looked. "Isn't that enough?"

Lights burned late at Finkster's office that night. "It's this way," said Finkster, fighting a cloud of depression. "Linden Thackeray has lost his fucking mind. Our great liaison with the common people, our man with the common clay still under his fingernails has forgotten who he is. He wants to make art."

Jim Knott shook his head. Art was an elusive goal, only reached by not seeking it. Knott hoped to make money. "He did have that fall."

"And that fall knocked a screw loose," said LuAnne Bessing. "But you guys told me he'd tightened it."

Finkster could see serious fluctuations in his bottom line.

"Orville Mayberry said he was back full strength." Jim looked at LuAnne.

"In three or four conversations," added LuAnne, on beam with Jim, spreading the blame around.

"Well, whoever said what to whom, the fact remains that Thackeray doesn't wish to soil his hands with the likes of Bubbles III."

"How does he wish to soil his hands?" asked Jim.

"With a piece of dreck called *The Eagle and the Dove*."

'Sounds like a stage-play," said LuAnne.

Finkster shook his head. "Even my wife wouldn't see something like that."

"What's it about?" LuAnne asked.

"The Pope meets a sorcerer in the alley and they talk about soap."

"The *Pope?*" Jim was shaken.

"Maybe it's funny," said LuAnne.

"Thackeray isn't smart enough to be funny. He's fart funny. It takes a real writer to write comedy and there aren't three of them in this town."

Finkster realized in the moment that this was not a situation to be dithered with. It took direct action. "What we're going to do is twist every arm we can reach. The highway, the by-way, and the back way. But we've got to get that idiot to change what's left of his mind. Got that?"

"Got it," said LuAnne.

"Got it," said Jim.

Chapter 27

A Life of Its Own

Meanwhile Quick and Leslie were at Pink's Hot Dogs. A Pink's dog tasted great if the world was with you, terrible and cheap if you were fighting the vicissitudes of life.

"Don't these things taste great?" asked Quick, indicating the wrapped chili-cheese dogs. Pink's had that very cool L.A. vibe. Once, at two in the morning, he had met the actor Forrest Whitaker in line. He had tried to interest the actor in a Michael Quick screenplay.

"Never heard of Michael Quick," said Whitaker. "You his agent?"

"No," said Quick.

"Are *you* Michael Quick?" asked Whitaker.

Quick read the actor's face. Whitaker was here to get a hot dog.

"Uh, no, I'm not," said Quick.

"Then fuck him. I'm here to get a hot dog," said Whitaker.

Quick had nodded his head. Self-disgust leaked bile into his guts. It was one thing for Peter to deny Christ three times before morning. You could build a church on that. But to deny yourself was a deeper level of shame and sin. He paid for his chili-cheese dog but had thrown it away.

"So Finkster liked your idea?" asked Leslie, drinking Dr. Brown's Root Beer.

"He warmed to it. At first I think he was a little set back."

"What did you tell him about Bubbles III?"

"Just what we discussed. That I didn't want to write it. That I didn't want to direct it. That I didn't want to produce it. That I thought we should aim for something higher. You've only got so much time in this life."

Leslie smiled at him. Dazzlingly. "You're my hero, Michael. Someone needed to talk to that guy and someone finally did. Congratulations." Leslie paused. "He's going to greenlight *Eagle and the Dove,* right?"

Quick nodded expansively in the affirmative. "Finkster and I are tight. I wouldn't worry about it." Man, these were good dogs. Pink's, baby.

He was trying to remember the salient points of *The Eagle and the Dove* the next morning when Anne Bullard rang his desk. Already? He'd only been in twenty minutes. "Orville Mayberry needs a minute, Mr. Thackeray."

Of course Orville Mayberry needed a minute. Orville's job seemed to be sneaking, spying, and probing. In Quick's lower moments, he wondered if Orville indeed worked for him. Anyhow, you couldn't let anyone bull their way into your private space. "Tell Orville forty minutes, Miss Bullard," he ordered.

Quick was lost in thought. Don Juan dressed in regular clothes wherever he went. Would the Pope? At a roadside diner? Or would robes be involved?

Mayberry, ill at ease, was led in by Anne Bullard. "If I may be so bold, sir, please let me ask you to reconsider your position on Bubbles III."

Quick frowned. Wasn't this outfit called *Thackeray Entertainment*? "In what way am I to reconsider my position, Mr. Mayberry?"

"Well, Mr. Thackeray," said Mayberry, "you've managed to foment a solid rapport with the public with the Bubbles franchise. In these risky times, it would be a shame to squander that rapport—"

Quick cut him off. What times weren't risky? "Did you say *squander*, Mr. Mayberry?"

"I meant dilute, sir." Mayberry was slick as synthetic motor oil. "It would be a shame to dilute your rapport with a left field entry. However beautiful it may be."

Lunch, two hours later at the Imperial cafeteria was similarly compromised. Ginger had been talking about broiled tofu in white miso sauce with a touch of rosemary when a young John Wayne-type had waved, smiled, waved again, and finally stood up to approach.

"Who is this guy?" whispered Quick. It was obvious Ginger admired the young man. Lean, muscled, handsome, full head of luxuriant hair.

"That's Oak Adams, CAA's new hope."

"Do I know him?" asked Quick.

"I don't think so," returned Ginger. "He has the biggest cock in Hollywood."

A shot of peccant disquiet ran over Quick's consciousness. "Wonderful. Do you know him?"

"Not personally."

Oak Adams reached their table. His hand was as big as a catcher's mitt. Quick's disappeared inside it. Like a fly and a trout.

"I've always loved your work, Mr. Thackeray," said the new hope, "but the Bubble movies especially."

"Why, thank you, Oak. That's nice of you to say."

"You're a genius, Mr. Thackeray. A stone genius.

"Don't embarrass me, Oak," said Quick.

"And I'm told that *Bubbles in the Tubbles* is going to be even better than the first two. I can't wait."

What was all the shit today about Bubbles III? It was getting sinister.

"Also," continued Adams, "I wanted to congratulate

you on the award nominations."

Award nominations? What had he missed? Ginger smiled at him from across the table.

"The Academy Award nominations were just announced." Adams looked at his phone. "Ten minutes ago."

Ginger looked at her phone. "You've been nominated almost in every category."

Suddenly, as if it had all been planned, all the diners in the cafeteria rose as one to applaud him. And then from the applause, a chant: "Bubbles III! Bubbles III! Bubbles III!"

Christ Jesus, thought Quick on the way back to his office, perhaps he had, mistakenly, of course, tapped into the mythical über-seele. Bubbles III had a life of its own. But it didn't matter. He would kill it with his bare hands.

By the time he rolled through the gates of Thackstone that evening he was exhausted. Within every single human encounter a reminder of Bubbles III had surfaced. A query, a comment, a congratulation. No peace. And now, while Quick enjoyed his second double-scotch by the pool, he watched Boother sidle up from the banana grotto.

"And how are we today, Linden?"

Quick was immediately irritated. He realized he had achieved the second stage of inebriation: bellicosity.

"Enough of this'we' stuff, doc. I feel like hell. I'm supposedly on top of the world. I have a company with a hundred and sixty-some employees. But everyone is trying to tell me what to do."

"Ginger says you drank like a fish at lunch today."

"What do fish drink like?"

"They're underwater."

"So they can't help it."

"And you're drinking now."

"So what?"

"Ginger tells me you told her you had nothing to do with Bu*bbles in the Tub*, or *Bubble Trouble*. And nothing to do with *Wrestle in the Ruffles*."

"I didn't. I had nothing to do with *Bikini Tiger*, either. Or that goddam *California Rubber King*."

Boother's head sank into his hands. "What about your politics of identity, Linden?"

"What does that mean?"

"What's your name?"

"It's not Linden."

Boother groaned.

"Imagine how I feel, doc."

Bertrando made an appearance. "You have call, Mr. Thackeray."

"Who is it, Bertrando?"

"John Webster Fennis, sir."

"Fuck John Webster Fennis, Bertrando."

"Yes, sir."

Quick and Boother watched Bertrando walk off. "I don't think you should let this attitude get out of hand, Linden. You have important work to do. Very important work."

"Oh, bullshit." Suddenly he felt sorry for Boother. "Look, doc, don't worry about me. I'll feel better tomorrow. And then I'll go back to pretending to your heart's content. I've got a new project I'm working on."

Boother brightened. "Bubbles III? I've heard really good things about it."

"Good *God!* Don't I get a moment's peace? I thought I told everyone but I guess I've got to tell you, too. I'm not doing Bubbles III. I'm *not* doing it."

Boother took a deep breath. "You know, I haven't mentioned this before, but there is another avenue of treatment we might explore."

"Nothing is going to work, doc. Believe me."

"That's the exact logjam this process is designed to address. It's called E-C-T."

"E-C-T." The letters brought nothing to mind. "What's E-C-T?"

Boother cleared his throat. "Electro-convulsive therapy."

"Electro-convul—shock treatment? *SHOCK TREATMENT?"*

Boother raised his hands. "Shock treatment no longer describes a modern, valid, careful, efficacious procedure."

Quick was never so sure of anything in his life. "Not to my brain, you don't."

"Just as electricity can restore rhythm after cardio-arrythmia, a precise micro-voltage applied to the—"

But those were his last words on the subject. Quick's foot gave Boother's chair a violent shove, and over the pool's edge went the good doctor.

Quick rushed inside and stamped all the way to his office where he picked up the phone, dialed Orville Mayberry. After a few rings his assistant picked up.

"Mayberry, this is Thackeray."

"How's the script coming, Mr. Thackeray?"

"Which script, Mayberry?"

"Bubbles III, sir. I'm told it's a masterpiece."

"A masterpiece."

"That's right, sir."

"How can it be a masterpiece if I haven't written a single goddam word?"

"When is a Linden Thackeray script not a masterpiece?"

"When it does not exist."

"Not a problem, sir."

"Not a problem?"

"No, sir."

"How is that not a problem?"

"Your track record is golden."

"I am not my track record. We're changing things this time."

"I'm all ears, sir."

"Then get this straight. Bubbles III is off the slate. I will not write, direct, or produce—"

"—those are not impediments, Mr. Tha—"

"Neither will anyone else associated in any way with Thackeray Entertainment write, direct, or produce Bubbles III. Am I making myself clear?"

"Substantially, sir."

"Substantially? What have you not understood *totally?* I want the entire operation shut down. Is that clear? The entire operation *shut down*. Period. Are you understanding me?"

"Yes, sir."

"What do you understand?"

"English, sir. You're not anxious to proceed with *Bubbles in the Tubbles*."

"*Nooo*. I'm not *not* anxious to proceed. I'm not *going* to proceed. Do you understand me?"

"Yes, sir."

"Good. Then make it so." Quick hung up as Boother and Ginger entered the office. He pointed a finger at Boother. "Get out. You're nothing but a witch doctor. Get out."

Boother extended his soft white hands imploringly. "Relax, Linden, relax. Ride out the emotional wave. Imagine a broad, white beach—"

Quick was having none of it. "Hey. Hey. HEY. Witch doctor. You're fired, witch doctor. FIRED. Shitcanned, let go, relieved of duty, shown the door, kicked in the ass. GET OUT. And take your electrodes with you. And your cauldrons."

Boother retired with a frightened Ginger snuffling by his side. Quick decided to call Leslie to inform her of his total victory. A windy paragraph into his recital she cut him off.

"Have you been drinking?"

Drinking? Yes. Hell, yes. To celebrate our victory. Against the low forces of sedimentary crap. Barbara Walters drifted hazily into his mind. She folded her hands, cocked her head and asked him to betray himself to millions. Tell me, Linden, she said. Tell me about the dwinking and the dwugth.

"Have you been drinking?" repeated Leslie, into his silence.

"Who's been dwinking?"

"You have."

"Dwinking?"

Damn, he'd said it again. "Drinking," he enunciated clearly, but the ball was already in play.

"Call me later when you're sober," said Leslie and hung up.

God damn it, fumed Quick. What the hell. How about a little support here? Tell me about the dwinking and the dwugth, said Barbara.

Morning found him with a savage headache. He knew his eyes were not filled with sand but it felt like it. Hell with Leslie. He'd take Ginger to Hawaii. Ginger was still snuffling at the breakfast table. He only could take so much. "Ginger, stop crying for godsake and pack your things."

But this was inadvertent gasoline on the fire. "Pack?" she wailed. She let out an ear-splitting shriek, threw her napkin into her eggs and ran off. Mrs. Alvarez gave Quick the fisheye. Everyone was against him. He found Ginger sobbing in her room, beyond reach of explanation. He was at wit's end until she lunged for his belt. Oh, well. Expertly she robbed him of all strength.

"Do I still have to pack?" she asked, nourished.

"Yes," said Quick. "We're going to Hawaii."

Chapter 28

At His Own Pleasure

The Cadillac limousine rolled smoothly toward LAX. Quick wished only to doze but Ginger was chattering away on a variety of subjects. Then she realized she was sitting on a remote. She turned to Quick. "Would you mind if I turn on the TV?"

He threw up a hand. "Please."

Up came Heidi Hogan and the F Channel on two monitors. "F Channel," said Ginger. "Heidi Hogan."

Quick opened one eye for his reconstructed fantasy love, always far beyond his reach. Suddenly it occurred to him that she was probably totally available to him now. A shot of sadness chastened him. Some fantasies were not meant to be fulfilled.

"Hi. I'm Heidi Hogan," smiled Heidi, "on special assignment for the F Channel. And the answer is, YES! You are now being effed! You are now having fun!"

A shot of Thackeray Entertainment came on screen. "There's your building!" shrieked Ginger, daggers into his eardrums.

"We're here live at Imperial Studios, where the spokesman for Thackeray Entertainment is about to make an important announcement," said Heidi. On screen, Orville Mayberry advanced to a podium on the front steps, a sheaf of papers in his hand. "Now, here's Orville Mayberry, personal assistant to Linden Thackeray," finished Heidi.

The camera pushed in on ambitious Mayberry. "Good afternoon, everyone. I'm Orville Mayberry, personal assistant to Linden Thackeray. As you all know, there's been a lot of speculation about a Bubbles III project. Today I talked to both Linden Thackeray and studio president, Charlie Finkster. Here's the straight skinny."

Quick opened both eyes. "Give'em the skinny, Orville, give'em the skinny."

Mayberry smiled into the camera. "As of noon today, Imperial Pictures and Thackeray Entertainment have agreed to go ahead with a Bubbles III project tentatively named "Bubbles in the Tubbles."

Quick's eyes fell out of his head.

"Linden Thackeray, the genius, will write and direct a Finkster/Imperial production. I've read a few pages of "Bubbles in the Tubbles" and it's just plain hilarious. It's great. Up to the usual Thackeray standard. Bubbles fans will not be disappointed." Mayberry straightened his papers. "And that's all, folks."

Ginger looked over at Quick, eyes wide. "I ... I guess you changed your mind."

Quick was incapable of speech. His head pounded with rage, pain, humiliation, and non-understanding. The limousine had almost reached the airport. He directed it back to Imperial Studios.

By the time he pulled up in front of Thackeray Entertainment, his red rage had subsided into a cold, hard, black, deep anger. He walked up the steps, threw open the thick green glass door. The security guard started to say something, Quick cut him off.

"You're fired." He walked past the guard, firing everyone he came across. Like a postal worker with an unlimited magazine. He fired high, he fired low. He fired in the copy room, he fired at the coffee mess, he fired in the executive suite.

Quick grinned like Blackbeard with a hold full of

teenage virgin queens. The entire establishment was in an uproar, spilling into the hallways, spreading their hands, shaking their heads. He was looking for Mayberry when Mayberry found him. "May I have a word with you, sir?"

Quick was incredulous. This Mayberry had chutzpah. "What about two words? You're fired."

Mayberry just stared at him. "A word in private, sir." They went past a solemn Anne Bullard and Stacy Green to Quick's inner office and shut the door.

"What is it you don't understand?" continued Quick, "I told you, last night, as plainly as possible, to shut down Bubbles III. Yet you countermanded my direct order. *My direct order.* And then you went on fucking TV and lied out your ass."

A pause followed. "Were you drinking last night, sir?"

Quick felt his eyes bulge, his incredulity stretched to new horizons. "And what the HELL would that be to you if I was?"

Mayberry just stared at him, a tinge of melancholy about the eyes. A silence yawned. Something was very, very wrong.

"Is there something I don't understand?" asked Quick.

Mayberry nodded. "Yes, sir. You better talk to Charlie Finkster, sir."

Quick walked across the lot in a fog of doubt and foreboding. Who was Mayberry *really?* And who was Michael Quick? He straightened his shoulders and tried to display confidence.

Finkster's secretary, Marguerite, was full of good cheer. Finkster was equally jovial. "Well, well, well, Linden. How's every little thing?"

Quick was more than a little perplexed. Things were

not well. Things were not well at all. "How is every little thing? I just fired one hundred and sixty-five of one hundred and sixty- seven employees of Thackeray Entertainment. That's how things are." He had spared Anne Bullard and Stacy Green.

"That was rather rash, don't you think?"

"It may have been. What am I not getting? What's with Orville Mayberry? Don't I run Thackeray Entertainment?"

"Of course you run Thackeray Entertainment. Your name is Thackeray, isn't it?" Finkster smiled and turned to a cabinet behind him, opened it. A bottle of Early Times became visible."Would you care for a little whack of Early Times, Linden?"

"I can take it straight, Charlie. The truth, that is."

Finkster sighed, turned, steepled his long, manicured fingers. "The truth." Finkster pursed his lips. "The truth is, Linden, the truth is you can't fire someone ... who technically doesn't work for you."

"So my employees, therefore, aren't my employees." Quick felt his heartbeat in his face.He thought further. "I get it. They're Imperial's employees. *Your* employees."

"That's right, Linden. Most of them. They've been on loan. From me to you. We, uh, never thought it would come to this."

Quick nodded woodenly. Though only recently taking possession of the company, he felt bereft. "How many employees do I really have?" It would be best to establish the bottom line.

Finkster cleared his throat. "One."

Quick laughed aloud. "One. I've got one employee. Who is the poor bastard?"

Finkster cleared his throat again.

Quick suddenly understood. "It's *me*. I'm the only employee of Thackeray Entertainment."

"That's right." Finkster interlaced his fingers on his desk. "But you serve entirely at your own pleasure."

Quick was an ass, but he was his own ass. Of what he was better than, he was unsure. "And the nine projects on Thackeray's slate. I'm not sure what they are exactly, but where does *The Eagle and the Dove* stand among them?"

Finkster beamed. "Now you're talking, Linny, now you're talking! They're going to be great, I know it. And *you* used to know it. And I know you'll know it again. We can hardly wait."

Quick waved a restraining hand. "I'm serious, Charlie. Where does *Eagle and the Dove* stand among these products?"

"First on the list. First and foremost. Right after Bubbles IV through XII."

Quick felt as unsubstantial as a ghost.

Finkster led him to the door. Finkster's arm went around his shoulders. "Don't worry about a thing, Linny, it's all under control. Every aspect signed, sealed, and delivered. Your services to us, ours to you. We've got it made in the shade."

Quick was numb, a dull visitor in his own head. He said something and Finkster nodded and smiled.

Finkster stopped in the doorway. "Look. Take the rest of the afternoon off, go down to my club and relax. It'll be good for you. A good massage, a haircut, a shave, a manicure, a blowjob—you'll be a new man. The Oscars are next week, Sunday. I'm betting you'll do well."

Chapter 29

Thackeray Daiquiri

The week leading up to the awards found Quick thickly inebriated. He had argued with Leslie and again felt friendless and alone. Now he sat in his library with his Wrist-Rocket slingshot, a sack of ball bearings, and a bottle of Early Times. Across the room was his Best Original Screenplay Oscar for *Bubbles in the Tub* which he had brought back from the office. All the fired employees were back the next morning and their presence embarrassed him deeply. He aimed and fired and Oscar took one right in the forehead. The impact made a small but satisfying sound.

Every now and then a distressed Ginger would look in, shake her head, implore him to snap out of it. She had no idea how deep it was. PING! Another direct hit on Oscar. Dr. Boother's entreaties were similarly ignored. Quick refused to think of a broad, white beach, a clear open sky, or a deep blue sea. He suggested to Boother, whose employment he had reinstated, that the doctor have sex with a duck.

He loaded the Wrist-Rocket and fired. Another good shot. This one ricocheted off stoic Oscar and hit the power switch for the eighty-six-inch television.

On came the Channel 7 afternoon news with Saul Croyer. "That was Debbie Michaels on the red carpet at the Kodak Theater," intoned the anchorman, basso profundo. "Now we turn to Heidi Hogan, at the Old Director's Home in Pasadena. The Old Director's Home just received a substantial gift from gifted filmmaker and current multiple Oscar nominee, Linden Thackeray. Heidi?"

Heidi smiled brilliantly into the camera. "Thank you, Saul. And yes, I'm here at the Old Director's Home, with the Home's oldest resident, Brander Morley."

An ancient creature stood beside her in a mis-buttoned shirt. Posture and age put his eyes directly at boob level and rendered him cute. Heidi beamed down at him. "Mr. Morley, what do you think of Linden Thackeray's substantial gift?"

Morley cupped his ear. "Who?"

"Linden Thackeray. Linden Thackeray and his substantial gift."

"Linda who?"

"Lin-den. Linden Thack-er-ay," said Heidi, enunciating every syllable.

"Never heard of him," said Morley, plucking the microphone from Heidi with surprisingly strong fingers. "Of course, my first picture was *Pistol Harvest*."

Heidi was unprepared for the theft. How dare you, you moth-eaten old shit-eater, she thought. She reached for the microphone, a reporter's equivalent of a policeman's weapon, something not to be relinquished.

Morley hung on, turned his shoulder. "Then came *Peck o'Pistols*, of course."

A struggle for the microphone began in earnest. Heidi's ear monitor was ripped out, her good humor going with it. "Give me my microphone, Mr. Morley," said Heidi.

Morley stamped on her foot. "Then came *Night of Many Pistols*, in 1943," he rasped. "And I remain open for offers."

News director Bud Cameron switched to cam 2, cued Saul Croyer. Croyer smiled professionally, turned to gaze at the monitor where the struggle continued.

"Heidi? Heidi, can you hear me? What is the nature of the substantial gift?"

Heidi grabbed the microphone, Morley grabbed a big breast and hung on. "Heidi," said Croyer, "can you hear me? What is the nature of the substantial gift from gifted filmmaker Linden Thackeray?"

The reporter and the old director went down in tangled heap. Croyer addressed the red light. "Our apologies. We're experiencing some technical difficulties at the present time." He touched his earpiece, as if listening. "I'm told that the substantial gift to the director's home is half the profits of director Linden Thackeray's Thackeray Daiquiri Mix. Thank you, Linden Thackeray. Thank you, Heidi Hogan."

Quick turned down the TV, turned to Boother. "When did I invent the Thackeray Daiquiri, doc?"

Boother knocked back a hydrocodone tablet with a Diet Squirt. "The Thackeray Daiquiri? You had nothing to do with it," said the doctor.

Quick fell to his knees and laughed and laughed and laughed.

Chapter 30

Eleven

Later that afternoon, on Hollywood Boulevard, a limousine deposited Quick and Ginger at the foot of the red carpet leading into the Kodak Theater. Behind ropes, fans waved excitedly. Many were blowing bubbles. He waved, they waved. He was getting the hang of it.

How did it feel to be nominated for eleven awards? asked Debbie Michaels.

Though mystified as to the nomination protocols, Quick was humble and grateful. He wished only the best for the other candidates. He was happy just to be there.

How was *Bubbles III* coming?

A masterpiece still on training wheels.

The Thackeray Daiquiri Mix wasn't so bad, either, Quick decided. Since he was living in a dream, he'd decided to make the best of it. He'd downed three daiquiris by showtime and was feeling good. He and Ginger were in the fourth row, central, on the aisle, when his name was called.

"And the Oscar for Best Costume Design goes to ... to Linden Thackery ... for *Bubble Trouble.*"

The dream continued. Cameras turned to him and thousands of eyes as well.

Ginger, hugely excited, elbowed him. "Get up there. You won."

I won? I won what? Part shock and part daiquiri, fully impaired.

"Get up there," Ginger hissed. So he did.

On stage, Oak Adams clapped him on the back, shook his hand, gave him the Golden Man. A game-show curtain-girl-type in a long, white formal white dress pushed him to the microphone.

A billion and half people leaned into their televisions and waited. "Uhhh... uhh... thank you," he said vacantly. He remembered other memorable Oscar speeches. There weren't many he could recall at the moment. You really like me, I want to thank my lawyer, I'm the king of the world. And those weren't appropriate. "I, uh ... I want to thank," he paused, longly.

Who would he thank, after all? He didn't remember if he had done anything in the first place. "Uhhh ... I want to thank," again he foundered, but a conclusion surfaced and he clutched it gratefully, "I want to thank ... everyone who helped me." There. Simple, to the point, disappointing a few, offending no one.

Finis.

Curtain girl led him offstage where he was circuitously recycled to his seat by Ginger. "Jesus, Linden," she whispered, "you looked like a zombie up there."

"I feel like a zombie," he said, trying to draw healing oxygen through his liver. Then they called his name again.

Barry Manilow was on stage. "And the Song of the Year is," he tore open the envelope, "Bubbles Two by Two." By Linden Thackeray, *Bubble Trouble*." A sea of applause floated him to the podium. Manilow hugged him like an old friend from Brooklyn, handed him the prize of a lifetime.

Quick was feeling more at ease. "Thank you. Thank you." He nodded right and left. "I want to thank the

Academy." People always did that. He raised the statue in the air, pumped it up and down. Who else helped with a song? That was it. Musicians. "I want to thank all the musicians." That went over well. He extrapolated, "Musicians everywhere." He'd found a theme. "Musicians 'round the world." A couple more nods and pumps and the music came up and another curtain-girl led him away.

He'd been back in his seat for only two or three more awards when, again, he was up for another.

Centerstage was a lady who reminded him of Meg Ryan. "And for Best Visual Effects ... the Oscar goes to ... Linden Thackeray. *Bubble Trouble*!"

"Thank you, thank you, thank you." He looked from right and left, from orchestra to balcony, waved his shiny prize. "I want to thank the Academy." Then he spied Finkster applauding politely in the third row. "With a special thanks to my man, Charlie Finkster." Finkster rose to standing ovation and a good portion of the crowd followed his lead.

After a brief daiquiri respite, lightning struck again. And again. And again and again and again. Film editing, art direction, original score, sound mixing, sound editing. Best makeup made nine. He had to put the Oscars in an empty cardboard liquor box at his feet. The backstage press corps were all over him, white on rice. Then, like a bowling pin, he knocked over Best Director. He pumped the Oscar until he felt his rotator cuff. Then he walked backstage, waved at Heidi Hogan.

Heidi, broadcasting, waved back. "What a night, Saul, what a night. And it belongs to Linden Thackeray, who just waved at me. *Ten Oscars,* Saul. An unprecedented feat. No one else has managed more than three. And he has ten! With the big one, Best Picture, just around the corner. And of course, Linden's in the running."

Linden got back to his seat just as the applause for Russell Crowe subsided. "Now, demonstrating that the Academy is not entirely blind to comedy," said the Australian star, "here's a clip from our fifth candidate for best picture, *Bubble Trouble*. Take a look."

The screen lights up to depict:

A couple, Ed and Tipper, 45 and 28, sit in a hot tub underneath bright, bright stars. Only their heads are visible, the water is smooth, almost still.

"You've told everyone but me, Ed. My father, my mother, my sisters."

Ed is happy and relaxed. "Told them what, Tipper?"

"Told them how much you loved me. Cherished me. Adored me."

"But you know how much."

"I do know. But I want to hear you tell me."

"I think I can do that."

"Then do it, darling," says Tipper, her voice velvet. "Tell me how you feel when it's time to come to my bed. Tell me."

Ed's face is suffused with deep emotion, the intense look of love. Then a loud RUMBLING is heard—BUBBLES bobulate to the surface, disturbing the still water.

Tipper stares at Ed for an incredulous second. "You rude son of a bitch! How dare you? That isn't funny!"

She comes at Ed with her nails, trying to scratch. They both disappear below the water, finally reemerge.

"Okay, you win," Ed says, still grinning, holding her wrists. Then his face grows serious. "But you know what really isn't funny?"

"What?"

Ed lets go of her wrists." Global warming. It's

ruining the world."

"You can say that again."

"Global warming. It's ruining the world."

Tipper laughs." I didn't mean to really say it again, silly." She pauses, her eyes fill. "And what about the children?"

Ed shakes his head. "Think of them. By the tens of millions. Sleeping under polluted skies. On straw."

"Wet straw."

Ed and Tipper gaze at one another. Ed reaches for her, kisses her. "I love you."

Tipper looks into his eyes. "I love you, too." They kiss again. "How much do you love me, Ed?"

A loud RUMBLING is heard – BUBBLES bobulate to the surface.

The screen goes dark, lights come up, applause thunders. Crowe is laughing, too. He waves the coveted envelope." And the winner, for Best Picture," the envelope is opened, "the winner is... the winner is *Bubble Trouble*! Producers Linden Thackeray, Charlie Finkster, and Orville Mayberry!"

Quick found himself carried to the stage by his colleagues and in that moment all doubt vanished. He realized for once and for all that Michael Quick was a figment of his imagination. He was, indubitably, Linden Thackeray. Linden Thackeray the tremendous winner. Linden Thackeray, back in the round. Linden Thackeray, a perfect sphere.

After brief comments from Finkster and Mayberry, Linden approached the microphone. The standing ovation was deafening. He bade them sit, but they wouldn't. Finally they did. Linden wiped the sweat from his brow. "I'm electrified, I'm mystified, I'm petrified ... and I'm stupefied. There are no words for this. Thank you. Thank you. *Thank you.* I thank the Academy once again." He waved, a Nixon-big-arc-side-to-sider and walked off the stage. The cheers followed him, a physical pressure.

Backstage, Linden found himself with Ginger, Finkster, and Mayberry, surrounded by a huge media knot. Mics and lights bobbed and loomed, questions flew like arrows. Finkster leaned close to Quick, grinned. "Well, Linden. How does it feel? How does it feel?"

Linden shook his head. They said, in great movies, the hero struggles and struggles and finally makes himself whole. Never had those words meant more to him than in this moment. The feeling was the best he'd ever felt in his whole life. Hail the conquering hero. "It feels good, Charlie. It feels great. Feels like I'm home." Linden paused to enjoy the sensation. Then he turned, grinned at Finkster. "Feels so good, Charlie, it's like it was fixed."

Finkster smiled, slapped him on the back. "Oh, it was."

Chapter 31

Lucky Franklin

Three minutes later Michael Quick stepped through a back door into a drizzling rain. In his arms he carried the cardboard liquor box with his eleven Oscars, a world record. His liver had done its work, he was sober. Intensely sober. There were parties all over town, of course. Where he would be the lion. But he never felt less like partying than at this moment. Of course, his reluctance could be overcome with three hits, three shots, or three lines but his heart wasn't in it. With his cellphone he called a taxi and slipped anonymously into the backseat.

"Where to?" asked the cabbie.

"Just drive." The drizzle suited him fine. Down Hollywood Boulevard. Through Thai-town and Little Armenia. 'Til Hollywood's union with Sunset Boulevard. Down, through Silverlake and Angeleno Heights to downtown. Past City Hall, past the Times building. Past the Original Pantry. Past Grigson Putty. Past MacArthur Park. Swinging up to Wilshire. Past Lafayette Park. Past the noble edifice that had been Bullock's Wilshire when Caucasians lived downtown. Past the Wiltern Theater where B.B. King would perform in the next week.

The rain came harder as the taxi moved west past the tar pits, through the Miracle Mile, and into Beverly Hills. Passing Kate Mantilini's he realized he was hungry. Which meant, against all inclination, he would continue to live.

The cab circled back, Quick gave the guy a nice tip.

Quick had always liked Mantilini's, both as himself and his extended self, Linden Thackeray. It wasn't until the shot of Early Times was warming his gullet that he remembered the Oscars. He'd left them in the taxi. Oh, well, like little lost sheep, they'd find their way home. Like little lost fixed sheep.

No other patrons seemed to have noticed him there, alone in his booth. He ordered a bowl of split pea soup and a cheeseburger. Pride had prevented him from calling Leslie but now he was sorely tempted. Pride was not good eating. She answered on the third ring.

"Hey, it's Michael," he said.

"Well, well, well," she said in a pleased voice. "Historic Mr. Eleven. Congratulations. How are you?"

"The Awards are fixed."

"No, they're not."

"Oh, yes, they are. They most certainly are."

"How are you?"

"Terrible."

"Why?"

"Everything. Look. I want to see you. I miss you. I really miss you. Can I come over?"

"Let me ask Franklin."

Shards of ice penetrated his heart. *"Who's Franklin?"*

"Somebody great. I think you'll approve."

"You met someone?"

"Met him on Melrose. He followed me home. He got lucky. Real lucky."

Christ Jesus. Lucky. Already. She'd been a peach, just waiting to fall off the branch. All the time he'd wasted on the Candy Lee Jopsies of the world. Thinking Leslie would always be around. And now some lump named Franklin had entered the picture in a big way. It served him right. "Well, Franklin's very fortunate."

"Oh, he knows that." Lucky Franklin thumped his

tail on the linoleum and went back to licking his balls. "So when are you coming to see us?" asked Leslie, scratching Franklin's ear with her toe.

Quick was on Desolation Row. "Oh, one of these days, I guess. Soon, I promise." He couldn't take any more. "Good night, Leslie." He clicked off, set the phone down, stared out on rainy Wilshire Boulevard. He'd blown it. He'd blown it. There he sat with a thousand dollars cash in his pocket, and credit cards entitling him to all the pleasures of the world. Yet he had nothing. Wanted nothing. Wanted to be nowhere in particular.

He realized someone was standing by his table. He looked up. A devastating beauty in a green silk dress stared down at him. Half Irish, half Filipina, a goddess in the flesh. "Hi, Linden," she said in the tiniest voice.

"Hello," said Quick.

"Linden?" she repeated.

"Yes?"

"You don't know me, do you?" Her voice was utter sadness.

Quick looked at her. "I wish I did." She was beauty. He needed beauty at the moment and he knew how to play the game. She extended a hand, Quick took it, kissed it. "I'm Irene," she said.

Quick looked tragically into her pellucid green eyes. "Hello, Irene." He'd always loved the name, Irene. Pretty soon her pants would be off.

Irene stepped closer. He could smell the fragrance wafting from between her breasts. "I want ... I want to give you something, Linden."

He was ready. He was more than ready. "Then give it to me … Irene."

Eyes never leaving his, Irene withdrew an envelope from her bounteous bosom, passed it to him solemnly.

Quick took the envelope. Irene's approach was a

new one. "What's this, darling?" he asked.

Suddenly Irene's voice lost its tantalizing bedroom appeal. It became harsh and Brooklyn-like. "Yer soived, Mr. Thack'ray. Compliments of John Webster Fennis." That said, she turned on her heel, walked out.

Quick sat there, took a deep breath, tried to think. But his mind was a blank. Impressions feathered to the surface but dissolved. He opened the envelope.

John Webster Fennis, representing all five of his ex-wives, was demanding a five-fold increase in alimony for each. Quick rubbed his eyes. He had reached the center of a perfect circle of intolerability. It was suicide or inebriation. He went to the bar, had three quick whiskies. But even that was temporary solace. But where would he go? What should he do? Then he saw himself on television. Followed by the number eleven. Heidi Hogan, muted, smiled her way through her report, which finished with a shot of the Hollywood sign.

Quick paid up, got up to leave, the bartender called after him, waved an envelope. "Yo, you forgot this." The bartender slid the envelope down the bar. "Looks important."

John Webster Fennis. Quick explained. "Five ex-wives all wanting more alimony. Just one lawyer, though."

"Five?"

"Yup. Five."

"Christ."

"You said it."

"You were a serious optimist."

"I was indeed."

"And they're all getting that alimony."

"All of them. And they all want more."

The bartender shook his head. "Not me, man. I'd hang myself first."

And there it was.

The solution to everything. The rightness of it flowed over him like cool water. It was self-evident. His head was clear and clean. It was so simple. It was absolutely right. He had not married five grasping women. He had married Clara. God, he had loved her. And missed her still. The world he was in was patently not real. So he would leave it. Just the way he came in. His eyes filled with tears.

"You alright, man?" asked the bartender.

"I'm perfect," Quick replied. "Call me a cab, please." He pulled up Leslie on his cellphone and dialed.

"Hello?" said Leslie in a sleepy voice.

"Leslie, it's Michael again. Sorry I'm calling again."

"That's okay. Is something the matter?"

"No. Everything's alright. I'm going to be taking a little trip."

"A little trip? Where to?"

"It's hard to explain, since I'm not sure. But I can't stay here."

"You sound like you're about to do something stupid."

"I want to tell you one thing before I go." He paused. "I love you. And you'll always be in my mind."

"This sounds very stupid. You're scaring me. Where are you going?"

The bartender caught his attention. "Yo. Your cab is here."

"Michael? What are you doing?"

"Leslie, my cab's here. I have to go. God bless you. Have a good life. I love you." He hung up. Walked towards the door and his cab. Then he stopped, walked back to the bartender, opened his wallet. He counted what he had. Twelve hundred dollars. He segregated ten hundreds and slid them over to the bartender.

"What's this?" the man asked.

Quick smiled. "That's your tip."

It was counted. "This is a thousand bucks, here, buddy."

"I know what's there. Don't spend it all in one place."

He stepped out into the night air, climbed into the waiting cab. He passed two hundred dollars to the cabbie. "Take me to the Hollywood sign," said Quick.

BOOK II

The Patient of Dr. Singh

Chapter 32

Artifice and Intention

It should have been the highpoint of Linden Thackeray's career. Yet when he looked upon the morrow it was ashes, simply the advent of yesterday. Something was perfectly wrong, polished, beautiful and wrong, and he was powerless to correct it. He had sampled every single pleasure life had to offer. Drugs, drink, women, art, sport, travel, triumph. Slowly the life he had built so carefully, brick by brick, had imprisoned him totally and completely. He was bored and feeling dangerous to himself.

Finkster and Imperial were almost in his pocket. Nine more films. With his new deal, he would be recompensed richly and deservedly until he was into his sixties. But if he had nothing to live for now, for what would he be working then? Mentions in Beautiful People columns, Viagra and the company of strangers? He was fucking bored. And angry.

Money was to a man what beauty was to a woman. To the degree it existed it fostered insincerity and mendacity.

Now wealthy, his essential character, what he hoped to be loved for, had been rendered inconsequential. His need for connection, still paramount and desperate, created his own willful blindness as to the motives of those whom he charmed so easily.

Now age was mixed into the formula. Since assumption of true and adult personality, around seventeen or eighteen years of age, Thackeray felt that a man never changed inside. The same appetites, the same joys, the same disappointments. The same appreciation for pretty faces. But, at forty-three, young women regarded him with a natural distrust and suspicion. He was not of their tribe. His motives and motivations, his music, his humor, were all different from their own.

Yet, all of these realities had been swept aside when he met Sarah Roswell. Brunette, very pretty, twenty-four, a dental assistant in the lair of Dr. Tobiashi, purveyor of the $17,500 Hollywood root canal. Should bicuspids ever come up, Sarah would have an informed opinion. Sarah made him laugh. Unprepared, his breath had been taken away.

Of course, this had happened before, but this time his hopeful heart declared it new and unique. Sarah was too young to be impressed, she hadn't known who he was, had no knowledge of his accomplishments. Her affections flowed *including* the gray at his temples not in spite of it.

The fact that he had a girlfriend, Ginger, living with him at Thackstone, didn't enter the equation. Ginger was a pleasant, if transparent, social climber. Her thinly disguised ambitions lay wholly within his next film, *Bubbles in the Tubbles*. Which, of course, would make ten zillion dollars. If love proved real with Sarah, Ginger would have to go. He was capable of such distinctions, and capable of acting upon them.

Driving home from Imperial in his Bentley convertible, savoring the late afternoon breeze, he concocted the idea that led him, later that night, to the Hollywood sign.

He would surprise Sarah. With a visit. With a visit and a fistful of roses. A visit, a fistful of roses, and an invitation to breakfast—in London or Paris or

Amsterdam. Her wild, trusting heart rewarded for its pure and girlish grace.

He was standing at the address board, flowers in hand, ready to ring her apartment when a women exited, opening the door for him. Now the surprise would be perfect. He would appear unannounced.

"Those roses aren't for me, are they?" asked the woman. She was about forty.

"If only I had known," said Thackeray, gallantly. The woman was attractive on the tragic cusp of wilt. *C'est la vie*. There was no way around aging.

The elevator whisked him to the fourth floor. An open walkway accessed the apartments and overlooked the blue pool. Approaching 4B he heard voices. Sarah. Sarah and somebody.

"So you gotta real thing with this old dude, is that it?" A male voice.

"I've seen him. I'm *seeing* him. He's a nice guy."

"Does he think you're in love with him?"

"I'm not responsible for what he thinks."

"Is he in love with you?"

"Of course, he is." Sarah's voice was clipped and businesslike. "They all are. "

"What does fucking Tobiashi put in his fucking anesthetic?"

"I don't know. But it works."

Thackeray stood, paralyzed. She couldn't be talking about him. Could she be? He watched her curtain flutter in the wind.

"What about us?" challenged the man.

"I'm tired of living on dreams, Sean."

"I'm the best fuckin' writer in this town. You know that. Things'll turn around. They have to."

"I'll get him a script. I told you I would. And I will. When the moment is right."

"When the moment is right."

"Yes. When the moment is right."

A pause. A silence.

"Tell me you don't love me, Sarah. Tell me."

The flowers slipped through Thackeray's fingers. Finally, after frozen seconds, he managed to unroot himself, to turn, to walk without seeing, down the stairs, through the lobby, out the front door.

That night, sober in the face of a thousand choices, he realized he didn't care if tomorrow came. He searched within himself for folly, found stony ground. He had done everything. Fifteen times. Then, around a long forgotten mental corner, a dream of his youth was recalled to him.

He stood high on a precipice overlooking a vast city of lights. After some interval of painless waiting, he had calmly stepped into space. He remembered the swelling joy as he did not fall, instead moved ahead on a seamless, smooth plane of transparency and well-being. For a second, his recollection seemed to include companions. He tried to sort out the particulars but his effort corrupted the reverie and it fell softly to pieces, defying reassembly.

Thackeray took a deep breath. He had just figured it out. He would get the big Mercedes, and after a stop at Laurel Hardware, he would drive to the Hollywood Sign.

Chapter 33

God

In the darkness came a vibration. A rumbling. Continuous. But not repetitive. Then slowly, as consciousness came on line, he separated from the vibration, realized the nature of the distinction.

He opened his eyes. He hurt all over. And he was … in the back of a moving ambulance. Or what felt like a moving ambulance. Who was he? Why was he here?

A mental snapshot: looking up at the Hollywood sign. That's right. Ass that he was, he had considered suicide. Another snapshot: the dive toward earth. No. *No.* Had he really done something so stupid? That didn't sound like... Linden Thackeray. *His name was Linden Thackeray.* And he had tried to commit suicide. A thornish pain seemed to penetrate his spine. And his suicide had failed.

Ass.

Or had it failed? Maybe pain was after-image. The phantom limb of life. His mind seemed to be working very slowly. Where was the white light? The sensation of overwhelming love? Where was the tunnel? Maybe the ambulance was the tunnel. He was dealing with new realities here.

Then he realized he was not alone. A man, a huge man, with a huge head, a huge bald head, a black man with a huge bald head sat motionless, facing away, paying him no attention at all.

Through the pain it occurred to Thackeray that perhaps this was God.

GOD ... the locus of first thought. The root of human experience. The father of time and distance. And so amazingly in tune with modern Hollywood standards for God – anything other than a white male. Well, they'd finally got one thing right.

His head hurt like hell.

Then God turned, looked into his eyes. "You one stupid son of a bitch. What's your name?"

"Linden Thackeray." A whisper was all he could manage.

The Creator checked something on His clipboard, shook His head. "You sure about that?"

Thackeray felt himself deflate. Maybe the soul had a secret name, unknown to crude consciousness below, like the Hebrew name of God. "I think it's Linden Thackeray. I mean, it always has been."

The Source of All was unimpressed, scratched His ear. "How you feel?"

"I guess I'm okay," Thackeray ventured. Evasions would be transparent. "My back hurts. And my head. How am I, really?"

"Why'd you jump off the sign?"

God got right to the point. As HE would.

Why indeed had he jumped? Under present circumstances it seemed preposterous. "I don't know. It seemed like a good idea."

"You lucky to be alive."

"Am I ... am I alive?" inquired Thackeray.

"Damn straight you are. This is ain't no dream. Creditors up your ass?"

Earthy. God was earthy. And astral creditors? With what did you pay interest? Part of his soul? Had he squandered his only true resource? "Where are you taking me?" Thackeray blurted. His soul had spoken.

There it was. He had boldly asked the ultimate

question. Now he waited on judgment.

The Absolute finished some paperwork, picked His teeth with a pen. "You goin' to Hollywood Presbyterian."

Chapter 34

Blue Smock and Friends

Hollywood Presbyterian, of course, was out of the question. Not in this life. Though he had entered the world there forty-three years ago, the neighborhood had changed, the old hospital now resided in seedy East Hollywood. Neighboring residential hotels still advertised STEAM HEAT. On unreinforced brick walls that survived earthquake. Take me to Cedars, he had demanded.

At Cedars, two soulless medical record technicians asked for proof of insurance. At his direction, they looked through his wallet. From their expressions, they found nothing to please them.

"Nothing here, Mr. Quick," said a Filipino in a blue smock.

"Who's Mr. Quick?" asked Thackeray.

"The guy on your driver's license."

"Bullshit. My name is Thackeray. I've been in and out of this place three times. Last time you pinched my gallbladder. I don't know who the hell Mr. Quick is. That isn't my wallet, obviously."

Blue Smock read the license again. As if it were possible to make a mistake reading plain English. *Michael James Quick. DOB: 06-04-1965.* "When's your birthday, sir?"

Thackeray sighed. "June 4th, 1965." Blue Smock was giving him a look. "And that says?" asked Thackeray.

"It says June 4th, 1965," said Blue Smock.

There was an odd coincidence. He tried to shake his head but that made his neck hurt. "My name," here he paused, "is Linden Thackeray." Every syllable diamond hard.

Usually deliveries of this nature were followed by dawning recognition and profuse apology. This time two blank stares were offered. "Christ Jesus," said Thackeray, "don't you guys ever go to the movies?"

"Every once in a while," allowed Blue Smock.

"Not while I'm at work," said his friend. He was also in a blue smock.

I'm surrounded by idiots in blue smocks. Each one with some narrow, obtuse specialty. One knew pliers, the next knew thimbles. "You guys ever see *Bubbles in the Tub*?"

Blue Smock II shook his head. "Never heard of it."

Later, a hospital administrator, Mrs. Arden, came to visit his cubicle in emergency care.

Mrs. Arden leaned over him, smiling a professional smile. This was the imbecile who'd jumped off the Hollywood sign. Who claimed to be a famous writer, "How are you, sir?" she asked, a sheaf of papers in hand.

Thackeray, stiff as a mummy, tried to draw a calm breath. "Finally. An American from America who's been to high school."

Mrs. Arden's eyes got a little frosty. "Carlos and Juan are both fine Americans, sir. And outstanding employees of Cedars-Sinai."

Thackeray realized he would need this woman's cooperation. "I'm sure they are, ma'am, but if they don't know a few of my movies they're not culturally literate. Nothing against them personally." He pushed a smile to the front of his lips. "I'm sure you'd know them."

Mrs. Arden looked at her papers again, then the patient. "You say you've been treated here before."

"Three times."

"Under what name?"

Christ. Maybe they gave out free diplomas when this woman had been in high school. "I was treated under my own name. Writer's Guild insurance each time."

"And your name, sir?"

"Thackeray. Linden Thackeray."

The woman's eyes were unresponsive.

"I wrote *Bubbles in the Tub?* And *Bubble Trouble? Tiger in the Ruffles? Bikini Tiger*?"

"If those are adult movies, sir, I wouldn't have seen them." She stood straighter now.

Thackeray searched the ceiling. He had fallen into little Appalachia on San Vicente. "I won an Oscar for best screenplay for *Bubbles in the Tub.* That doesn't ring a bell?"

"No, sir. It does not."

"How about *California Rubber King*?"

"How do you spell Thackeray, sir?"

He spelled it. Twice. But the system didn't acknowledge Linden Thackeray. Christ Jesus. He'd have to call Ray Anderson in the morning, have the lawyer kick some doctor ass. Hell, he'd call Anderson now.

Mrs. Arden tapped her foot through the several attempts to reach Ray Anderson. But the firm Anderson, Tobin & McKean didn't seem to exist any longer. Finally, after finding his social security number a fiction, a cold request for cash was made.

Thackeray would have torn his hair out had he not been restrained by bandages and splints. Somehow, in significant ways, he had ceased to exist. Even his own phone number, active just hours ago, now belonged to an annoyed stranger. He had examined the driver's license of Michael James Quick. If he didn't know better, it was him. Height, weight, hair color, birthday.

Stiff, sore, and on the edge of deep fright, he promised resolution on the morrow and begged for rest.

Mrs. Arden seemed to acquiesce. He had no sooner closed his eyes when he was roused by a cadre of smocks. "We're moving you, buddy," they said.

"Moving me? Who says? No way. I need a private room. I insist on a private room."

"He *insists* on a private room," parroted an insolent smock.

Two other smocks, large and black, encouraged him towards a wheelchair. "This will all be straightened out tomorrow," he begged, trying to resist. But no one could see reason and no one accepted bribes on credit. Now he would be forced to share a room with some tragedy-ridden old screw and his drip-drip, huff and puff life-support equipment. Forced exposure to the truly ill. And their nosy, snuffling relatives. Where the hell was Ray Anderson?

The elevator into which he was rolled was moving too fast and dropped too far.

"Where are you taking me?"

"Another hospital."

"What?"

"Another hospital."

"Another hospital? No way."

"Yes, way."

"Christ Jesus. I won't go back to Hollywood Presbyterian."

"Don't worry about Hollywood Presbyterian."

"Good."

Pause. "Where *are* you taking me?"

"County/USC."

"County. County/USC? But that's where..."

"Yep. That's where they take the people who can't pay nothin'."

Chapter 35

Dr. Singh and Estelle

At County/USC Thackeray sank into his bed in Ward 13. Gratefully, he closed his eyes and let the Vicodin do its business. Tomorrow he would attend to other matters. And perhaps the world would right itself and he would wake up where he belonged.

◆ ◆ ◆

Dr. Singh, from Benares, looked at the white man across his desk. Mr. Quick had turned out to be quite a problem. In the parlance of baseball, Dr. Singh's passion, Mr. Quick had hit for the cycle. His jump from the Hollywood sign had induced wounds of *all five kinds at the same time*. Contusion, abrasion, laceration, compression, and puncture.

But it had also given his patient grand delusions. Now he was a rich, celebrated director/producer with an Academy Award under his belt. He lived in a mansion in Beverly Hills. He had five ex-wives, a live-in girlfriend, and a staff. He had a production company with several hundred employees and a slate of films to produce.

Exercising due diligence, Dr. Singh had searched the internet. Of course, there was nothing there about Linden Thackeray. He had found another Thackeray, a William Makepeace Thackeray. Who had written a book called *The Rose and the Ring*. Dr. Singh was unfamiliar with the effort. In any case, Mr. Thackeray died a couple of centuries ago and had not been heard from since.

"How are we feeling today, sir?" asked Dr. Singh, adopting a neutral tack.

Actually, Thackeray had never felt more wretched in his life. Though the mirror assured and reassured him of his identity, his fingerprints said, without question, that his name was Michael James Quick. Who he absolutely was not.

Yet maybe he was. If he were very, very, very ill. Because the world he was in now did not contain a movie called *Bubbles in the Tub*. Imperial Studios did not exist. Charlie Finkster was not president of Imperial. Imperial did not exist. Orville Mayberry wasn't his personal asshole at Thackeray Entertainment. Because Thackeray Entertainment did not exist either.

"Physically, doc, I'm better than I was." He liked this doctor from India. Doc Singh wasn't building his financial portfolio at his expense. "Am I schizophrenic?"

The doctor spread his hands. "Of that, I am not sure. It is a mysterious world in which we live, whose purpose we do not understand. However, as you undoubtedly realize, there can be no grand conspiracy against you."

The doctor fingered some papers on his desk. "The tests say your cognitive skills are unimpaired. Yet, for some reason, you have adopted an alternate personal history, an alternate world history. Honestly, I've never heard anything like it."

An alternate world history. That about said it. Thackeray was totally lost.

"But perhaps this all may be shock-related. Let's give it a week and see what happens."

But every morning the mirror reflected Linden Thackeray down to the last pore he could see without glasses. He was Linden Thackeray. He *had* to be. He *was*.

Yet, none of the phone numbers he could remember reached anyone he knew. Not a single one. He was getting no better. Thursday, in session, Dr. Singh told him to expect a visitor.

"A visitor? Who?" Thackeray was overjoyed. Now he fully comprehended the essence of visiting the afflicted, why these visits were considered a good work by all the major religions. Something he had never quite gotten around to doing.

"Your girlfriend is visiting," smiled Dr. Singh.

The information was cool water to his parched soul. Ginger! Where in hell had she been? He'd kick her rear end, but only after smothering her with grateful kisses. Neighboring mendicants offered advice. Brush your teeth. Floss. Comb your hair. Ditch the paper slippers. Shave.

Paper slippers. Did anyone *need* to be told? Certain aspects of public hospital life were just not acceptable. Fabricated from the same parsimonious stock as the ass gaskets, known to supply officers as toilet seat protectors, the only gait suggested by the paper slipper was the slow, pitiful shuffle. The rubber ward rumba.

In a way paper slippers were coal mine canaries. If someone wore them, that person was unwell. Four beds down, Crazy Looga coveted his slippers, along with all those he could pilfer, hiding them carefully under his mattress. Looga had whittled down the English language to one word: *looga.*

At two-fifteen he looked up to see a strange woman staring at him from the foot of his bed. It wasn't Ginger.

In a green apron that said *Ask Me About Lumber,* the woman looked distressed. She couldn't be the one coming to see me. Please, no.

"Michael?" she said, taking off some formidable glasses, peering. She looked as if she'd never had sex without gloves and napkins. No *California Rubber King* for her. Where was Ginger, his red-crested-double-breasted-mattress-thrasher? Maybe this woman was mistaken.

"Can I help you, ma'am?" He prayed she was lost.

"Michael, how are you?"

His heart sank like a cement kite on a windy day. On the other hand, she was the only human being in the world whose concern, mistaken or not, was not professional.

"I don't know how I am," he replied, honestly, "but thanks for asking."

They made their way to the visitors' lounge. Looga gave him a grave thumbs-up as they went by.

"You don't remember who I am," she said, sitting on an unsteady orange chair. "Do you?"

He searched every feature of her face. "No." A silence followed.

"Did you jump off the Hollywood sign?"

"I'm pretty sure I did."

"Pretty sure?"

"I don't recall exactly. But people claim to have seen me."

She paused a moment. "Was it because of me?"

Thackeray could find no cause to blame her, blame anyone. "No, it wasn't."

"Thank you, Michael."

Thackeray nodded. "You're welcome. I guess."

"What do you remember, Michael?"

Which meant there was something to remember. Undoubtedly bad decisions in bad light. Most men had ruined their lives that way. He coughed and began. "First, I want to thank you for coming to visit me. What do I remember? Nothing. Tell me about us."

"We were boyfriend/girlfriend."

"I see." He would avoid re-recruitment.

"But we broke up." She would avoid re-recruitment.

"There must have been reasons." He would absolutely avoid re-recruitment.

"There were." She would absolutely avoid re-recruitment. "Do you call yourself Michael?"

"I call myself Linden Thackeray."

"Oh. You're going up in the world. Getting hoity-toity."

"You've never heard of Linden Thackeray?"

"Never heard of him. I'm Estelle, by the way."

"Hi, Estelle."

"Hi."

He would try to learn something about himself. "What was I good at?"

"You were good at your job when your ambitions didn't carry you away."

"What ambitions?"

"You were always trying to write."

"*Trying*. Did you read anything?"

"I tried. They were pretty thick."

If he had indeed been Linden Thackeray, producer, here was his comeuppance. He had often refused scripts on the *plop factor*: how hard they plopped on his desk from a height of twenty-four inches. Anything significantly over a hundred and twenty pages was usually written by an amateur. It plopped with suspect force.

"And the subjects were thick, too."

"Thick like what?" He was becoming annoyed on behalf of his other self.

"You know. Life, pain, fate, love. Stuff like that. Soggy stuff. I begged you to go light."

"Soggy."

"I begged you to go light. Put in a laugh here and

there for the folks."

"I refused?"

"Every single time."

"Are you a writer?"

"Of course not. I work in hardware and garden."

"Do you sell perineums?" This was his little joke. Geraniums, per*in*eums.

"If they're in season we probably do."

"I see."

Perineums were always in season. Strike one for the Rubber King.

"I think they're right near the magnolias."

If you say so. "I'm told they seldom see the light of day."

"Is it one of those flowers that smell bad?"

"Often it is."

Estelle breathed in and out through her long narrow nose. "I can probably get your old job back, Michael. If you're interested."

"What did I do?"

"You worked at Grigson Putty. In the enclosure department."

"Grigson Putty?"

"On Benner Street. In the enclosure department."

"What happens in the enclosure department?"

"You put lids on cans of putty."

"On cans of *putty*."

"On one-pound cans."

"I put lids on one-pound cans of putty *for a living*?"

"See! You're still ashamed."

"Ashamed? I'm—"

"You're ashamed. I can hear it in your voice. You were always ashamed. But it was something you were good at."

"I was good at it? Who wouldn't be?"

"There's that attitude again, Michael."

Michael. She'd called him Michael so very naturally. Maybe he was, truly, Michael. For the first time his complete soul was plunged into the frigid waters of doubt. Tears filled his eyes. He didn't know who he was. If you didn't know that, what else meant anything? Reality lay in shards on the floor.

◆ ◆ ◆

Later he discussed the Estelle meeting with Dr. Singh.

"You recalled nothing?" asked the doctor.

"Nothing. She was a complete, total stranger."

"You had been intimate?"

"I got that impression."

"That is unfortunate." The doctor corrected himself. "I mean that not recognizing her was unfortunate."

"Equally unfortunate," amended Thackeray. "She offered to help me get my old job back. What she said was my old job."

"What did you do?"

"Apparently, I was an enclosure technician."

"That sounds scientific," nodded Dr. Singh. "India herself is becoming a scientific powerhouse. What are the duties of an enclosure technician?"

"You put lids on one-pound cans of putty."

"Well, that's ... interesting," said Doctor Singh, finding the good foot. "And there's always room for advancement. And it's a good start."

"A start toward what?"

"Your life recovery. Have you forgotten you're to be discharged next week?"

Thackeray's mouth fell open. "Doc. You gotta be kidding. I'm not ready."

"No one ever is. And it doesn't mean the safety net

is totally withdrawn. We'll find you a bed in a group home. Or a hotel."

A downtown flophouse. He could smell the thin, stained mattress. That had borne the weight of ten thousand hopeless nights and a million bastard dreams. "But I'm really not ready, doc, I'm not ready. I don't who I am."

"We don't have the resources here for you, Mr. Quick." Dr. Singh used the patient's name on purpose. "You must reengage with life, sir."

The doctor was not unmoved by the plight of his patient. But the flood of patients would not, could not, be diverted. They were swept to his gates hourly by the ceaseless current of misfortune. Mr. Quick was one of the better off.

To a degree, no one knew who they were. We live inside a game, the doctor thought. In a way he admired unapologetic drunks. Signs claiming wine research. Trying to dilute reality into homogeneity, into something you could laugh at, into something that fit. Maybe we have a thousand lives in which to perfect ourselves. Or maybe we don't. He reached over his cluttered desk to shake Mr. Quick's hand.

Chapter 36

Grigson Putty, Honest Work

Then one day Thackeray returned from breakfast to find his bed stripped and his cardboard placard gone. He was now a graduate. Looga waved sadly from the dayroom.

Estelle picked him up and skeptically gave him a ride to Beverly Hills. Where he hoped he would find Thackstone. There wasn't a trace of it. Instead, reflecting architectural whimsy and hubris, he found a modern structure full of tiny, long windows set at odd angles in odd-shaped slabs. Somewhere, though not apparent to the common man, must have been a door.

"You *lived* here?"

The structure provided no rest for the eye. He wasn't sure what non-Euclidian geometry was, but this was probably an example of it. "No," he shook his head, "I never lived here." It was the final nail. Beautiful Thackstone had existed only in his mind. Beautiful Ginger and her throatsome proclivities also neurons adrift.

The next day he started back in at Grigson Putty. Thackeray's immediate supervisor was Ed Strickman. Immediately and instinctively he loathed Strickman. From pocket protector to receding hairline. And Strickman had it in for him, that much was obvious.

"You remember why you were fired, Mr. Quick?"

"No."

"Then how do I know you won't do it again?"

"I guess you don't."

"I'll be watching you. Like a hawk."

"Fine. I take it you weren't responsible for hiring me back."

"Damn straight I wasn't."

"I guess that means you don't hold much power around this chickenshit outfit."

Strickman's eyes bugged.

"So I'll tell you this," continued Thackeray. "I must have been easy on you before. But this time I'm going to file if you even look at me funny. Got it? I'm on a special program for retards and I won't be putting up with your bullshit. Now where's the guy who's going to show me my job?"

Strickman's gums flapped in outrage for a long second. "Follow me," he choked.

Thackeray was lead back downstairs, into the fill room and towards a huge machine that belched and farted and rattled and hummed, finally terminating in a long series of roller bars. A black man in his fifties was standing there.

"This is Neff," said Strickman, "as if you really don't remember. Maybe he'll help you out." Strickman stalked off.

"Welcome back, Hollywood," said Clay Neff, with a big smile, extending a palm to be slapped.

But at Thackeray's hesitation Neff withdrew his hand. "You don't remember me."

Thackeray looked at him. "I'm sorry. I don't."

"Clay Neff," said the black man. They shook. "We were pretty good friends."

Somehow, in total opposition to his feelings about Strickman, he felt instant comfort and comradeship with Clay Neff.

Neff laughed. "Lemme show you what you're going to be doing, Hollywood."

"That's it?" said Thackeray, seconds later.

"That's it."

Thackeray was dumbfounded. Even Estelle's description sounded more involved. His new career was checking that the big machine shat sufficient putty into one-pound cans as they went under the fill nozzle. Then he pounded a lid on with a mallet. A can came down the line every 5.3 seconds. He looked at Clay Neff. "This is really it?"

Neff shrugged. "What can I say? It ain't rocket science."

"It's not human."

"It remains honorable, though."

Thackeray nodded. Here was the honest dollar at land's end. Who did he have to fuck to get fired around here again? "Strickman told me I'd been fired. How do you get fired from this job? What did I get fired for?"

"Suspicion of smoking shit at breaktime. With me."

"Was the suspicion justified?"

"Oh, yeah. Totally and completely." Neff laughed ruefully. I had a joint bout as big around as my finger."

Neff's hands were enormous.

"But what difference could it have meant?"

"No difference."

"Do you have another one?"

Neff grinned.

In the alley, Thackeray appraised his alleged co-conspirator as Neff told him the rest of the story. The pot was pretty good. Downtown pot. Gangster pot.

Break ended, Neff concluded with his thanks and a handshake. Apparently, Quick had been a lidder who had loyally fallen on his own sword. Neff was a mixer. Eighty-five percent ground chalk, fifteen percent boiled linseed oil. Which should roll easily in the hand without exuding oil. Who knew?

The river of cans took his mind away and next thing he knew the river stopped and Bud Hunt, introduced as the facility manager, was slapping him on the back.

Hunt was corpulent, stuffed into his clothes, and florid of face. A term came to Thackeray's mind from his Navy days. *Bullop*. Ten pounds of shit in a five-pound bag.

"Glad to have you back, Quick." Hunt looked at his watch. "It's eleven-forty. Lunchtime. Fast Eddie'll be outside, as usual, for your morning burrito. Today it's on me. Keep your nose clean and we'll do fine."

As he ate the burrito, Thackeray had a feeling that he had been hired back to avoid a lawsuit over driving him to suicide. Various strangers paid their respects, welcomed him back.

"You for real jump off the sign, dude?" questioned someone named Osvado. "Da chronic?"

Thackeray shrugged. "Don't remember that much."

Osvado grinned. "Da chronic right there, bro. You think you fly."

The day dragged on in a Zen trance. Hammer up, hammer down. Hammer up, hammer down. There was a break in the afternoon, and finally the last bell rang. Hammer up, hammer down.

Chapter 37

Hunter Baldwin

Estelle gave him a ride home, where he found a green envelope in the mailbox. Which he recognized as a residual check. It was for an effort he'd never heard of. *True Love/Black Death.*

Regardless of her disdain, the Writers Guild had squeezed out some money from some ex-communists in eastern Europe. Pay up, assholes. Eleven hundred dollars and change. And hmmm ... it was only five years late.

The nick-of-time check brought him current with his landlord, and got his car, a 1969 Cadillac Coupe de Ville, out of the impound yard on Fuller.

He'd never driven a Cadillac before. He filled the tank and was almost broke again. Twenty-six gallons. But the power and size were intoxicating. In his imagined life, if that was really what it had been, he had been rich and he had driven expensive automobiles. But now he tasted the upward contempt of the working man for pencil pushing pantywaists in Peugeots. Don't mess with the Motor City, motherfucker.

Thackeray had taken reluctant possession of Quick's literary efforts on the premises. Bored, he read them. They weren't half bad. They were quirky and personal. Hard to sell without a really good agent. *The Eagle and the Dove,* for instance. The Pope meets Don Juan at a roadside diner in New Mexico. Great conversation ... but who would pay to see something like that?

No one. That's why Quick was a lidder at Grigson.

Could he *possibly* be Quick?

That night a knock at the door interrupted a Man-Sized Salisbury Steak TV dinner with mashed potatoes. He opened the door to see a gorgeous redhead with a heroic bosom. Staring deep into his eyes.

"Are you Michael Quick?" she asked.

"Uh, maybe. Why? I don't have any money." He tried to keep his eyes focused on her face.

"I don't need money."

"Uh ... what do you need?"

"I need to know if you're Michael Quick."

"I guess so. What about it?"

With that she extended her hand to his chest, pushed him back into his living room. "I'm Hunter Baldwin," she intoned breathily, "and you're the greatest writer alive."

"Come on in," he said.

No sooner had the door shut behind her than long, shapely fingers undid the buttons on her blouse. It fell to the floor in an orlon whisper. Revealing God's beneficence.

"Do you like these?" she asked, cupping the gravity-defying marvels.

Next thing he knew she was kneeling before him. Thackeray glimpsed the promised land and arrived shortly thereafter. He opened his eyes to see her staring up at him, a smile on her face.

She drew the back of her hand across her mouth. "You're about to win a major award."

"Really. What award? I didn't know I was up. You know, for anything."

"I know something you don't know," she chided, wagging a finger.

"What would that be?"

She spat in the potted plant. "The Valley Theater

League has had its eye on you."

"The who?"

"The Valley Theater League."

"Never heard of them." Of course, he'd never heard of anything.

"The Valley Theater League is a group of theater-minded individuals devoted to theater in the San Fernando Valley and adjacent valleys."

"Adjacent valleys. Very commendable," said Thackeray solemnly. "Where do you fit in?"

"I'm the roving goodwill ambassador."

"Welcome," said Thackeray.

Chapter 38

The VTLAs

Hammer up, hammer down. Weeks passed like molasses. Some days he was sure he was and must have been Michael Quick, other days he believed in Linden Thackeray and the works of Linden Thackeray. Even if the internet made not a single mention of Thackeray or his works. His confusion was profound but he stuck to the basics. Hammer up, hammer down.

His relationship with Clay Neff had broadened into friendship. And Estelle would come by every so often for a cup of coffee, tell him details of their past. They had once taken a trip to Fresno to see a pluot, a recent grafting of plum and apricot. Thackeray pointed out the new fruit could well have been called an aprilum, but Estelle did not think that was funny. Nor had it been funny before.

Then came notification from the Valley Theater League. The Valley Theater League Awards were to be held at the Beverly Garland Hotel, formerly a Howard Johnson's Motor Inn. The site overlooked the freeway in Studio City. As Linden Thackeray, he had been to the mountain, he had won an Oscar for Best Original Screenplay.

Yet, as the VTLAs approached, he found himself hoping he would win. He was up for Author—Best New Play. Documentation was scant and neglected to mention for which work he was to be possibly celebrated. He searched the cluttered apartment and found notes referring to an anti-war effort, written in one single long session fueled by amphetamines. His handwriting was very similar to Quick's. Which was astounding—or not.

No title was mentioned in the notes.

He arrived at the ceremonies an hour early. Other starving writers and actors had arrived earlier and decimated the Costco buffet. All that was left were pickles, broccoli, and meat scraps on some beat-down lettuce. He wasn't that hungry anyway.

Then someone grabbed his arm. "Hi," said Hunter Baldwin, with a lurid grin, a VTL badge and a plunging strapless gown. "How's the greatest writer alive?"

"How would I know?" asked Thackeray, honestly.

"Come with me," she ordered.

"Okay. Where are we going?"

"You'll see," she said, briskly maneuvering through the throng. They moved into the lobby in the direction of the elevators. She pushed 4 and was silent through the ride. They exited into the hall and she pulled him down to 414. Once inside she engaged the deadbolt.

From the coffee cups, cigarette butts, and various papers, Thackeray gleaned that 414 was the temporary office of the VTLA. "Is there somebody I'm supposed—."

But Miss Baldwin pushed him onto the couch. In a trice, his pants were down and she was gobbling. After a bit he sighted the promised land and arrived grandly. She was on her feet in seconds. "Zip up, hombre, the ceremonies are about to begin." She pushed her hair around in the mirror, then turned to him, placed hand over heart, and began to solemnly recite:

Run rivers run red
Tonight tortured angels dead
Through shit through snot
For rich man's sons who struggle not
I march onward knowing this
I forge the stinking tides of piss
For thee

Thackeray stared at her with utter blankness. She stared back. Finally, he spread his hands.

She dropped her head and began to cry. "Am I that bad?" she asked, brokenly. "Am I that horrible?"

"Don't cry," he said, "you're wonderful."

"How could I be wonderful?"

"Your inner beauty is, uh ... it's always beautiful."

Recognizing inner beauty had often proved a reliable respite in emotional storms.

"What does my inner beauty have to do with it?" Her voice had acquired an edge.

Thackeray was truly lost. It was time to humbly admit ignorance. "I must be not getting something," he apologized.

"Shall I do it again?"

Thackeray was unsure of what she wished to do again. He was forty-three years of age and time was at the edge of the picture. "Uhhh, you needn't go to extraordinary lengths—"

"I'll do it again," she said.

"Uh, ok-ay. Suit yourself." Whatever was coming.

She cleared her throat, which worried him, but then extended her arms, recommenced her recitation.

Run rivers run red
Tonight tortured angels dead
Through shit through snot
For rich man's sons who struggle not
I march onward knowing this
I forge the stinking tides of piss
For thee

Thackeray flaffled in neutral, rubbing his hands. "Wonderful, wonderful."

"You're just saying that."

"No, I'm not."

"Don't patronize me."

"I wouldn't do that."

"You really liked it."

"Yes. Very much so. What exactly was it?"

Her eyes filled with flame. "You arrogant, egotistical *shit*. You bastard."

Thackeray was indeed lost at sea. "I'm so sorry. I can see I've hurt your feelings, but—"

"That's Oleander's soliloquy, you asshole. Are you pretending you don't recognize it?"

This time she accurately read his confusion. "You don't recognize Oleander's soliloquy?" Angered incredulity crawled over her face.

Helplessly, he shook his head. Oleander was a bush. Or was it a shrub? "Who is Oleander, please?"

She was now right in his face, enraged. "Did you just ask me who Oleander is?" Miss Baldwin fluttered and sputtered, a large vein throbbing on her forehead. Like a reptile. She'd been on her goddam fucking knees. "Is your name Michael Quick?"

"I believe so."

"YOU BELIEVE SO???" A vicious roundhouse whistled past his chin and her breasts flopped out of the strapless gown.

Thackeray ran for the door. It wouldn't open.

"I'm going to kill you," said the goodwill ambassador, lurching forward on stiletto heels.

He manipulated the deadbolt seconds before annihilation. "Put your gazongas back in," he yelled over his shoulder as he ran down the hall. He took the stairs and flew, reaching the lobby, looking for escape, just as another VTL official was going into meltdown.

"Where have you been, Quick? Your category is up next."

He was rushed to the Camelia Room. The smallish room was stuffed and brimming with expectation. "And now the nominations: Author—Best New Play," said the presenter.

Part of the crowd began to chant, *"Tides of Piss, Tides of Piss."*

And in opposition, equally lusty, *"Miss Butterley's in Love! Miss Butterley's in Love!"*

Tides of piss. A shot of alarm ran through his mind. Hadn't the fellatiatic ambassador mentioned such tides? Had he, Quick/Thackeray, in some way, fomented these tides?

The presenter leaned into the microphone. "Our first nomination, Daniel Cartwright, *Prison in the Sky.*" Cheers. Heads turned to whom Thackeray presumed was the writer. Cartwright waved a long patrician hand.

"Nancy Gables, *Miss Butterley's in Love.*" Miss Gables was a forty-some, tattooed, spiky punkette. The announcement met heavy applause.

"Thomas Pike, *Out of Kilter.*" Cheers for a large bearded man.

"David Hawkins, *Night Rhythm.*" More cheers. In a porkpie hat, with silver crosses hanging from his ears, Hawkins was the coolest man in the room.

"And finally, Michael James Quick, *The Tides of Piss.*" A sinking sensation fell over Thackeray, loosening his muscles. He wanted to sleep for two weeks. Why hadn't he written something harmless and light? A romantic trifle for the folks. Not *The Tides of Piss.* The play obviously meant something.

Meanwhile, opposing camps sought to out-shout one another.

"Tides of Piss!"

"Miss Butterley!"

"Tides of Piss! "

"Miss Butterley!"

The presenter raised a hand. "I just want to say, on a personal note, thank you Michael Quick, wherever you are, for writing this outrageous, courageous play. The war is immoral and illegal, a toy for the military/industrial complex. We should get the hell out of there right now. Lives are at stake."

The presenter, hand over heart, began his own recitation:

Run rivers run red
Tonight tortured angels dead
Through shit through snot
For rich man's sons who struggle not
I march onward knowing this
I forge the stinking tides of piss
For thee

A torrent of cheers and boos followed the excerpt, vied for supremacy. Heads turned right and left in search of the author.

People were crying for fuck's sake. Suddenly Thackeray was totally sure he was not Michael Quick. He couldn't be. What puerile vileness had Quick set to paper? And why had people paid attention? Quick was a lidder. Who gave a fuck what a lidder thought about war?

The presenter leaned into the microphone. "Let's see who wins." He opened the envelope, reached in, took the card, read silently, looked down. Then looked up, face neutral until he broke out in a wide grin. "And the winner, Best Author New Play... Michael James Quick."

An avalanche rolled over the Camelia Room. Thackeray felt a push at his back. It was the VTL rep. "Get up there. Get up there." People started turning to him, and he was propelled toward the podium.

Then he was at the podium, facing a wall of eyes in the din. "I would like to thank," his memory started to evaporate under the stress, the ... the, uh ... the league ... *what league*? "I would like to thank the league." But they seemed to want more. "Uh, and I would like to thank the San Fernando Valley," he added. "And adjacent valleys."

"We're gonna hang you, you yellow-bellied, red-assed, dick- smokin', shit-heel son of a bitch," shouted a failed Best Supporting Actor in a Musical nominee, "this is America."

"No, this is America," responded a professor-type, doffing the tweed coat, launching a bony fist. At that instant, as if by phase change, the crowd dissolved into mayhem, a sea of blows, curses, and shrieks.

A glass of something flew by Thackeray's head and crashed into the wall behind him. As he rose, hands protecting his head, Hunter Baldwin materialized, blood hunger in her eye, waving a lethal shoe.

"He's a ringer," said the goodwill ambassador, pointing viciously, "kill him where he stands!"

This was all Thackeray cared to witness. He ran toward a green exit sign, found the door beneath it, found his way down a narrow hallway and then he was outside. There was his trusty Cadillac. He ran toward it, vaulted over the door. It started up on the instant.

He stamped on the gas, angled for the street. He rolled through a thatchy hedge, destroyed a putting green, splashed out the koi pond, demolished the picnic tables, then slashed over the curb onto asphalt, and straightened out the vehicle with a screech.

All was quiet north on Vineland Avenue. The wind flowed softly up and over the windshield. He put his hand up, bathed his fingers in the laminar flow. A lazy moon, lying on its back, hung yellow in the sky above the San Fernando Valley. Thackeray exhaled a long, long breath. Of course, he had been victorious.

Chapter 39

Hammer Up

Hammer up, hammer down.

Grigson had passed beyond boring into true zen. A form of meditation. He no longer checked the cans for volume. There was no way the machine could vary from the standard dollop unless bubbles were involved. And bubbles had proved theoretical.

Hammer up, hammer down.

He saw why Quick had resorted to daily marijuana. He, as Thackeray, had early on abjured god's gift to working people. The principled young man he had been, briefly, had pursued natural transcendence through Transcendental Meditation.

A perfect fad, TM had mixed social optimism, secret knowledge, and a little Magical Mystery Tour Beatles gold dust. While practicing TM, allegedly, the lungs exchanged more oxygen, the liver released better enzymes, the brain connected more synapses, and lost libido was recovered and restored. And, it promised the nirvana of all sensations, the natural, repeatable high. When the internal dialogue surrendered to perfect nothingness.

Of course, inside knowledge didn't come cheap. After weeks of calm, seraphic instruction and the out-passage of two hundred and twenty dollars from his checking account, Thackeray was led to a small room dominated by a picture of the Maharishi Mahesh Yogi. Flowers were vased before his wise, smiling countenance and Thackeray's suggested gifts of fresh fruit and clean handkerchiefs were laid beside them.

"Now we are ready to begin," said his personal serene mistress, her breasts rolling largely beneath her robe of whitest white. Now he would receive his mantra, picked for him by the Maharishi Himself. It was a secret never to be revealed to another soul under pain of—well, under pain of something or other.

Thackeray looked around the tiny room. This very room, plain and unremarkable, unknown to him just months ago, was to be his portal to higher consciousness and the mysteries of time and space. How deeply satisfying. How solemnly ennobling.

"Your secret mantra," said mistress, "which you may never reveal, is *ah-ING-ga*."

Ah-ing-ga. It lolled on his tongue. Who could have guessed? The mellifluous simplicity. The weight of eternity and the enormity of fate and chance. Yes, his mantra was now his. What next?

"Now repeat your mantra, over and over," said mistress, her posture perfect. Her voice was a husky whisper, *"Ah-ing-ga, ah-ing-ga, ah-ing-ga, ah-ing-ga."*

Now Thackeray repeated the incantation. *"Ah-ing-ga, ah-ing-ga, ah-ing-ga,"* he enunciated softly. The tumblers to hidden and unknown locks were now seeking alignment. Soon all would be made manifest. *"Ah-ing-ga, ah-ing-ga, ah-ing-ga,"* he continued.

"Close your eyes," counseled the mistress, "and keep repeating your mantra."

He did as bid.

"Now silence the mantra, say it only within you, so only you can hear it."

Aha! It was not for dual consumption, another facet of the mystery. *Ah-ing-ga, ah-ing-ga, ah-ing-ga*. The syllables echoed down the corridors of his mind. Somewhere down the hallway, he knew, lay the jade revelation of ultimate significance, the jeweled elephant of absolute truth. *Ah-ing-ga, ah-ing-ga, ah-ing-ga* intoned Thackeray, inveterate explorer.

He proceeded thusly for several timeless minutes until he felt a touch on his wrist. He opened one eye. The touch seemed a tad premature. He had not yet caught sight of whatever it was he was to catch sight of. The small room was apparently the same small room.

The mistress smiled beatifically upon him. "There," she said. "Wasn't that wonderful?"

Driving home, Thackeray's disappointment was acute, vast, and deep. The check for two hundred twenty dollars had long since cleared, no doubt contributing to the Maharishi's ongoing serenity.

Yet, now, hammer in hand, he silently toasted his Transcendent Master. As the cans went by. The Master hadn't been smiling, he'd been laughing. Laughing did a lot for the liver, and it was good for the spleen, too. Cleared up the xiphoids, or whatever. Hammer up, hammer down.

Mantra in mind, the morning drifted by like a dream. Suddenly it was ten o'clock and Fast Eddie was outside selling his burritos.

He wondered if Fast Eddie had acquired a mantra. He doubted it. But it didn't really matter. He had found out that all the mantras for the fatted sheep were identical. Legions had *ah-ing-ga'd* in secret, jealous and compartmentalized. Yes, the Master had been laughing.

Clay Neff offered to share a fatty but Thackeray declined. There were some strange people down the alley. If he hadn't known better, they seemed to be looking at him.

When Fast Eddie returned for the lunch business, the two strange people had metastasized into three. The next day three were five.

Bud Hunt called him into his office. Strickman smirked from the corner. A copy of the *LA Times Calendar* section was open on the desk. "You the Michael Quick they're talkin' about here?" asked Hunt. "The revolutionary?"

The revolutionary? Thackeray looked at a picture of himself frozen stiff at the VTLA podium. *I want to thank the league. I want to thank the San Fernando Valley. And adjacent valleys.*

"*The Tides of Piss.*" Hunt looked up. "That's quite a title." Hunt tapped a pen on his desk. "What's it about?"

Thackeray remembered Hunter Baldwin's rendition of Oleander's soliloquy. "It's a love during time of war type thing. I think."

"You *think*? You don't know?" Strickman had brought the article to Hunt's attention.

"An author never really knows what he's writing about until long after he's finished." Especially if he had never begun. Thackeray's antipathy for Strickman had deepened with daily exposure.

"Then how does an author know it is finished?" Strickman's eyes glittered.

"It's not like making putty, Ed." Which, as everyone knew, was 85% ground chalk, 15% boiled linseed oil. "Writing is summoning all your humanity, all your history ... bringing them together at a single second to create something simple and true to life. And maybe even beautiful."

"That's the problem."

"What's the problem?"

"Remembering that putty is our business," said Strickman.

Hunt nodded. "It's putty that's important. We can't afford to lose focus."

Ah-ing-ga. Hammer up. *Ah-ing-ga.* Hammer down.

The day passed. He had no sooner arrived home than there was a knock at the door. He looked through the peeper's gate. He opened the door to the manager. "People been lookin' for you," said Bellrod, blowing his nose, scratching his gray face.

Thackeray had learned the manager was a Christian Scientist. Which meant he'd die of an untreated common disease and save Social Security thousands of dollars in the end. It took all kinds.

"What people?" asked Thackeray. Things were growing a little sinister around the edges.

"Question people."

"Question people?"

"Questions about this, questions about that. Questions about piss."

"Aha. Tides of piss."

Bellrod pointed a thick finger of acknowledgment then sneezed. "That was it. Your toilet's fine, by the way, isn't it? You ain't havin' no seepage, are you?"

"Seepage? What kind of seepage?"

"Loose bowl seepage. From a loose bowl. You'd know it if you had it."

Thackeray shrugged. "I guess I don't have any."

"Good. You don't want a loose bowl on your hands."

"Thanks for checking."

Later that night he answered another knock. A Mexican delivery driver handed him a vase of tired carnations and a pen. Thackeray signed, gave him a buck. He opened the card.

Congratulations, Tides of Piss. Your friends in the Truth Alliance.

By midnight he had three bouquets and a bottle of halfway good wine from Liquor Locker. The phone rang the next morning a little before six. "Is Michael Quick there?" asked a female voice.

"I don't think so," replied Thackeray, honestly, hanging up quickly. He had to be at Grigson by seven. The phone rang again as he locked the front door. The ride to work was uneventful until he turned on talk radio.

"*Tides of Piss* is a wake-up call to the nation," said listener Scott from Riverside. "The war is a disgrace and a travesty."

"You've got it all wrong, my friend," said the host. "*You* are a disgrace and a travesty. And this Michael Quick should be boiled in oil, then drawn and quartered. That's just for starters. Now, Maria, from Pasadena. What's up, Maria?"

"I'm an independent thinker and I just want to say ditto, ditto, ditto, ditto. Not just boiled in oil, drawn and quartered, but dipped in salt as well. Especially with troops in the field."

Thackeray noticed that a yellow car behind him had been on his ass for several minutes. A woman at the wheel. Boobs or bombs?

A slew of commercials commenced, he was in bad shape: his house loan was flawed, his credit debt should and could be restructured, his scalp could be repopulated, his teeth could be whitened by an average of nine shades, his erectile problems could be cured on the first visit, his carpets could be cleaned without soap, concerned strangers would find and deliver a soulmate for a small fee.

His speakers were sewer grates, filling his only means of transportation with shit, fatigue, and hopelessness. If this was the America that Muslims feared and reviled, he understood. Who would scrape through the muck to find Aaron Copland, Charles Ives, Jimi Hendrix, Muddy Waters, Willie Nelson? Who would find Robert Barrère the painter, Louis Menand the essayist, Preston Sturges, the filmmaker? Much less the millions of teachers laboring to educate the uneducable?

The radio host returned. Just because he had not served in the military did not mean his aggressive stance on the war was compromised. For eons he had yakked in the boonies for peanuts. He'd paid his dues.

Not everyone had the opportunity to carry a bayonet. Some Americans carried crosses of a different nature. His was a microphone, a cable, and the truth. Yes, Michael Quick had served his country in the Navy. Four years. At least according to findable documents. But anyone, if weak enough, could go rotten.

The Tides of Piss was rotten. Michael Quick, therefore, was rotten. What was wrong with boiling oil and salt?

Thackeray arrived six minutes before the hour at Grigson. An Eyewitness News van was already there, antenna up. Thackeray parked the Caddy, made for the employees' entrance.

"Are you Michael Quick?" inquired a telegenic specimen, displaying teeth six shades whiter than Tom Sawyer's fence.

Thackeray pointed out Armato Shade and Screen. "I think he works there, now."

Telegenic specimen looked at the cameraman, shrugged, eyed the screen shop.

Hammer up. *Ah-ing-ga.* Hammer down. *Ah-ing-ga.* The day had begun, floating on the Maharishi's groove.

He was regarded with new respect by his fellow employees, though most weren't sure just what he'd accomplished. What mattered was that TV crews were interested in him. "What you do again?" asked Osvado.

"I wrote a play," Thackeray explained, ignoring the unexplainable.

"Like TV?" Osvado remained unsure of the concept.

"Like Shakespeare," said Clay Neff.

"Not like Shakespeare," corrected Thackeray. How he wished he'd read the damn thing.

"Shakespeare," nodded Osvado, smiling. "Shakespeare lidder, too, maybe."

Obviously, there was no telling what Osvado may have understood. At lunch Thackeray made a statement to the gathered press. By three o'clock there were questions; was Grigson Putty patriotic putty? Could patriotic putty be made by anti-Americans? Could putty be sabotaged? Had Lionel Grigson been a member of the Communist Party? Who and what constituted Red Los Angeles? Who and what constituted Red America? Why was putty white?

Thackeray drove home on a full tank of gas and irony. His whole writing career had not stirred up five minutes controversy. He'd had a knack for the lowest common denominator and the talent to plumb it. Of pratfalls and flatulence he'd fashioned a handful of disposable symphonies. And now here he was, lauded and hounded for something that mattered. Of which he remembered nothing—because he was profoundly ill or because he was not the author. Piped if he did, hosed if he didn't.

Thackeray had not intended to write. He had intended to make money. One day, at traffic school, for a reckless-driving backwards u-turn in a school zone, he had been mistaken for a famous writer. He had shaken his head, smiled. No, I'm not Boyd Stuart. The woman pushed ahead on instinct. "You look just like him. Do you write?"

There are certain questions in life that are doors to someplace else. He recognized this as one of them. Write? "Uhh, *yes*. Yes, I do."

"What are you writing?"

What was he writing, indeed. Then he saw the traffic school blackboard. Filled with arrows, loops, and circles.

"It's an action piece."

"*Really*."

"I call it *Failure to Yield*."

That's how it began. Then one day someone decided his magnificent tragedy was funny.

Hey, you're funny. Dark funny.

After that he was funny.

Eventually came *Bubbles in the Tub* and an extremely stupid, totally ill-advised, long-term contract executed in post-Oscar euphoria. But now that slate had been wiped clean and indignant strangers were calling him a communist.

That night Estelle came to visit. "You're causing quite an uproar down there, Michael. They say you're a communist."

"I'm not a communist."

"That's not the point."

"What is the point?" Communism sounded good. Share and share alike, each according to his needs. The only hair in the ointment was human nature, full of envy, spite, pride, and self-inflation. As Orwell said, all were equal, but some were more equal than others.

Such a system was bound to fail miserably and it did. Success under those circumstances could have been predicated on one thing only: the great Linden Thackeray's benign despotism. Unfortunately for humankind, the revolution had come and gone without him.

"The point," continued Estelle, "is that you should consider distancing yourself from that play."

"Don't you have to read it before jumping to conclusions?"

"I did read it. Again. I still didn't get it."

At least she was consistent. He read it that night. He took exception to several overly florid passages, but the passion and directness could not be argued with. And the choice of words seemed uncannily familiar. All roads led to the grand conundrum. Identity. At the stroke of midnight four more floral baskets arrived and two bottles of champagne. Then came another knock at the door.

Thackeray eyed the knockee through the port, recognized her with some apprehension. It was Hunter Baldwin. "What do you want?" he asked.

The roving goodwill ambassador spread her hands. They were empty. "I want to apologize."

"Don't bother."

"Please don't be that way."

"Apology accepted. Go away."

"Please don't be that way."

"Why shouldn't I? You threatened to kill me."

"I was angry."

"That's not an excuse."

"It was a mistake."

She bent down below the viewing angle and disappeared, then reappeared with a handful of roses. "I brought these."

"Leave them on the doorstep."

"As a token of my sorrow and regret."

"Leave them on the doorstep."

"Please don't be that way. Please open up. I understand what I did was wrong."

"What is it you understand?" inquired Thackeray, allowing his mind to wander.

"I realize I'm not much of an actress."

"I can't help you with that."

"I also understand that the politics of identity are

deep and complicated. That in a way, we never know truly who we are. That names are only skin deep. That you were only trying to teach me the dichotomy between illusion and reality." She looked up from under heavy eyelids. "I also absolutely know you're the greatest writer alive." She paused. "And that you like my gazongas."

Thackeray opened the door. It was good to be king.

Chapter 40

Hammer Down

The week flew by and then it was next week Monday. Tuesday went by in a blur, culminating in questions about his position on organic farming.

His inquisitor was a grave, determined woman in a huge hat. From public television. Thackeray's last brush with agriculture had been an attempt at indoor marijuana farming during his college years. Years that may or may not have taken place. Regardless, his remembered efforts had met with failure. Seeds had sprouted under a spindly light and pleasant futures were contemplated until Vonnegut the cat ate the little verdencies. Resolutions of perseverance were uttered, but one by one the little clay pots broke and finally attrition was complete. The experiment was over.

"So you take no position on organic farming?" Big Hat asked in her trademark penetrating manner.

Thackeray spread his hands. "I don't know anything about organic farming," he replied.

Wednesday he was pilloried for his careless misappreciation of farmers and farm interests. Thursday he received the Lurdan Prize for Green Awareness.

Friday morning, right before first break, the Grigson assembly line broke down. Hammer up in anticipation, Thackeray watched as the fill nozzle farted instead of shat. Four cans went by in the new paradigm as he stared in startled disbelief. Ah-ing-oh-SHIT!

He watched his own trembling finger pause before hitting the mythic red button. Then he did push the red button. A bell rang, lights began to flash, and the giant machine shuddered to a halt.

Ed Strickman was immediately on scene. Putty flow had been interrupted and his mind was in shambles. Hands on hips, convinced of sabotage, he glared at Thackeray, eyes adagger.

The true culprit was the synchrony of a clogged filter, a relief valve wired shut, a weak O-ring and long lack of planned maintenance. The Looga Brothers Measured Filling Machine had been manufactured in 1947 for pie filling. Since 1966, and the bankruptcy of Hauser Pie, it had been chugging on, more or less on its own, unmolested, in the service of Grigson Putty.

There was nothing Thackeray could do. Because he himself had no discernible mechanical talent. Things worked for a while, and then they didn't. That was the way of the world. He watched the sad machines with dim curiosity as they croaked, screeched, whirred, and finally went silent.

Thackeray had known true mechanics. They were rare and born to their talent. They worked quickly, with instinct, insight, and empathy. The machines returned their solicitude with steady service. Such a man was needed now. Bert, the current maintenance chief, was not such a man.

Bert chewed his lip and lit a cigarette. "Could be a thousand things."

"If only Andrei were back," groaned Strickman, fingers in his hair, "he'd get it up."

Thackeray had heard of Andrei, the legendary, silent, lost genius of the Measured Filling Machine. One day Andrei had wandered off and had never been heard from again. He had never even collected his last paycheck. Slowly it dawned on Thackeray that he knew where Andrei was to be found.

Dr. Singh still presided over Ward 13. He did not appear surprised to see Thackeray.

"Hello, Mr. Quick," the doctor said affably, directing him into a chair. "Are you the Mr. Quick I've been reading about? The playwright of controversy?"

Thackeray shrugged. "I guess so."

Dr. Singh nodded. It was always easier to embrace success. "How are you?"

"Actually, I'm no better than I was. I don't think I wrote the play. But I'm dealing with everything."

"I'm sorry to hear progress has gone no further. Are you making friends?"

"Yes."

"Well, that's a good sign. Just keep trying." The doctor sat back. "Were you just in the neighborhood?"

"I've come to inquire about one of the guys on the ward."

"Who, may I ask?"

"Looga."

"You mean Andrei."

"Aha. I never knew his name. It *is* Andrei?"

"Andrei Konaslavsky.

"And he's still here?"

"He's still here. What about him?"

Thackeray smiled. "I think I know where he belongs."

Dr. Singh was a man of action. Thackeray, the doctor, and Looga departed within the hour, though Looga's pre-interview was not promising, The name Grigson Putty meant nothing. The name Looga Brothers Measured Filling Machine provoked no response. Ed Strickland's name dropped into the sea of consciousness with nary a splash.

But they went down to Grigson anyway. Ed Strickland and Bud Hunt were at lunch so Thackeray brought Looga right in. Looga recognized nothing until they entered the fill room. Looga stared at the machine. His hands came up then dropped to his sides. His eyes widened and a light was kindled within them. Uncertainty and confusion began a slow retreat from his countenance, replaced by dawning joy. The joy grew and grew. Tears escaped from the eyes that had now grown clear. He turned to Dr. Singh in gratitude. "Dr. Singh," said Andrei, in a low voice that achieved volume and clarity, "this is my machine. This is the Looga Brothers Measured Filling Machine."

For Dr. Singh, this was a moment he would remember forever. A moment he would relate to his many grandchildren thirty-five years later in Benares. A moment that made all the late hours, all the fat books, all the dull pencils, all the long travels in a strange land worthwhile.

"I saw, right in front of these eyes, a man recover himself. From years of darkness, from years in an unspeakable wilderness. Now, I did not," the old doctor cleaned his glasses with a handkerchief, "I did not cure him. A mind is too complicated for a term that simple. But I did lay the grounds for the miracle that took place. Oh, it was wonderful. Wonderful. I remember it as if it were yesterday. Wonderful." He cleaned his glasses again.

The fill room door opened and Ed Strickman walked in from lunch. Unknown people were in the plant and that meant trouble. And then Strickman saw Andrei Konaslavsky.

Strickman's mouth fell open. Words wouldn't come, though they were struggled for. Bud Hunt entered, realized whom he was looking at. "*Andrei? Andrei?* Is that you?"

"Andrei," managed Strickman, goggling, "where've you been?"

Andrei spread his hands, laughed. "I've been away.

But now I'm back if you want me."

"If we want you? Andrei, we *need* you." Andrei looked at Dr. Singh.

"Of course, you can, Mr. Konaslavsky," said Dr. Singh. "It would be the best thing for you. Details can be arranged. Nights at the ward, days here ... until all the details are worked out."

Andrei grinned hugely at everyone. Dr. Singh smiled. Thackeray smiled. Bud Hunt smiled. Ed Strickman smiled.

Strickman turned to Andrei after a glance at Hunt. On behalf of Grigson Putty, Andrei, we welcome you back. Your machine needs immediate work."

"Here I am," said Andrei.

"We still have the check we owe you," added Hunt.

"With interest, I suppose," added Thackeray, just for spice.

Another round of glances made the circuit. "Of course, with interest," said Hunt.

"Of course, with interest," said Strickman. "And one more thing." Strickman looked at Hunt. Hunt nodded quickly.

Strickman turned to Thackeray. "Speaking for Grigson Putty, Mr. Quick, you're fired."

Before the shock had time to register a new figure entered the fill room. "*Tides of Piss*, eh?" The stranger looked at the group. "Who's Michael Quick?"

Strickman pointed at his late employee. "He is."

Then everything seemed to happen in slow, inevitable motion. The stranger pulled a gun from his pocket, aimed it at Thackeray. "*The Tides of Piss* is a disgrace to this great nation," said the man and pulled the trigger.

Thackeray's world went black.

Chapter 41

The Hollywood Sign

His world recommenced an undefined time later. He was looking up at the ceiling, a circle of faces looking down at him. Dr. Singh was talking urgently to him, though Thackeray couldn't hear a word. But his mind was clear. *Ah-ing-ga, ah-ing-ga, ah-ing-ga, ah-ing-ga.* His mantra rose clearly to the surface. But for once, his internal dialogue, the endless chatter of consciousness, was silent. He was a translucent spirit, buoyed on the breast of time and space. His life was arrayed before him, in various circles and squares. His mother, his father, all the characters of his life. Then, across a line was another set of characters. Dr. Singh, Ed Strickman, Looga, Estelle, Hunter Baldwin.

Ah-ing-ga, ah-ing-ga, ah-ing-ga, ah-ing-ga. His name was Linden Thackeray. It could never be anything else. It could never have been anything else. It never *was* anything else.

Wherever he was now, wherever this was, he was a visitor. Further explanations were beside the point and beyond his comprehension.

Joining his two lives was the Hollywood sign. Thackeray smiled up at the circle. He knew, with absolute clarity, what had to be done. And what he had to do. What he *would* do.

BOOK III

The Feet of God

Chapter 42

The Significance of Putty

After leaving Mantilini's on Wilshire, the cab carrying Michael Quick reached the Hollywood sign twenty-seven minutes later. The cabbie scratched his head. "Not much going on here in the middle of the night, boss."

"Just the way I like it."

"Locked up, you know."

"I do know. Pull up right next to the fence. Right next to the fence. So I can jump over from the top of the cab."

The cabbie looked into the back seat. "Uh, are you sure you're feeling okay?"

"I'm okay as I've ever been. And you don't have to wait. You won't get in trouble. And I'll be careful on your roof."

The cabbie considered the two hundred dollars the crazy stranger had laid on him at Mantilini's. He'd put a blanket down. He had a packing blanket in the trunk.

Quick watched the cab's lights disappear. He turned, walked to the sign, removed tie and jacket and began to climb. He reached the top without undue difficulty. Again, he scaled the first vertical member of the letter H. He drew deep breaths and felt moisture at his hairline.

Below him Los Angeles spread into the distance in all directions. A town where he had been falsely coronated just that evening. And his only human connection to this alternate universe, Leslie had found another man. His breathing calmed. The air was soft and gentle. The moon was almost full. A deep peace fell over him. Then he felt a shuddering in the structure. He looked down. Someone was climbing up. Oh, Christ, couldn't a man get ten unencumbered minutes to himself?

"Don't jump yet, Michael," said a voice that was oddly familiar. Quick watched as the shadowed figure reached the summit. The man exhaled largely. "I'm getting a little old for this, buddy."

Quick recognized the voice. Astonishment raced through him. "Clay? Is that you?"

"Sure is, Hollywood." Clay slung a leg over, gathered his equilibrium, breathed deep.

"If you're really Clay Neff," Quick pointed, "then I'm really me. I'm really Michael."

"Course you are, Hollywood. Always have been."

A heavy layer of anxiety slid from his shoulders. It had been there so long he didn't even know he was carrying it. He was now five hundred pounds lighter.

Then a natural truculence surged forward. "So where the hell have you been? Knowing what you know? Knowing that I *didn't* know."

"I was back where you were."

"Where am I now?"

"A different place. A different universe."

Quick shook his head. "Well, no shit." He looked over at this old friend. "I won eleven Academy Awards tonight."

"Congratulations."

"Thanks."

They both laughed. Clay continued. "And thank you for falling on your sword back at Grigson. It takes a good human being do that for a friend."

Quick couldn't remember what he had done but

then he did. He shook his head. "It was the right thing to do, I guess. I didn't really think about it."

"That's right. You *didn't* think. You *acted* ... *with* and *by* the spirit. So, thank you, brother."

Quick shrugged, half sheepishly then grinned. A thought occurred to him. "If you're here, that means you can go back and forth."

Clay nodded. "That's right."

It slowly settled on Quick that Clay's mere presence was beyond astounding. "Why are you here, Clay?"

"To make sure things go right."

"And who are you?"

"That might be hard to describe in believable terms."

"Try me."

"I'm a necessary events facilitator."

"You're going to have to do better than that."

"Some people would call me an angel. Kind of, maybe. But actually, I'm a NEF."

"What's a neff?"

"A Necessary Events Facilitator."

"Oh. I get it. I thought your name was Neff. Which I always thought was weird."

"I *am* a NEF and Neff is my name. You know, for fun."

Quick nodded. "Right now, I think I could believe about anything."

"And I'll explain. But give me two minutes. Someone else is coming up."

"Someone else?"

A figure emerged from the darkness below. Quick could hear his heavy breathing. The man reached for the top, pulled himself the final distance up the second leg of the H. The moonlight illuminated his features and Quick nearly fell backwards. If he didn't know better, he was looking into his *own* face.

Clay coughed quietly, still startling the newcomer. "Don't jump yet," he said.

Thackeray looked over, saw Clay. He was as amazed as Quick had been. "What the *hell* are you doing here, Clay?"

"Waiting for you, son."

"He's facilitating necessary events," said Quick.

Thackeray realized there was someone beyond Clay. "What is this, a party?"

Clay bent, cupped his hands to light a cigarette, leaving Thackeray aspect to see Quick.

Quick waved, grinned. "I'm Michael Quick."

"Son of a bitch."

"Linden, meet Michael," said Clay, exhaling with satisfaction. There was nothing like rich Virginian tobacco in the entire multiverse. "Michael, meet Linden."

Thackeray didn't understand the full picture, but the pieces were there. And it was really nice to hear his own name.

"You know Clay, too?" asked Quick.

"Of course. Best mixer at Grigson."

"You've been there???"

Thackeray nodded. "Sure was. I was doing your job."

"You're a lidder."

"Yup. And a damn good one, too."

"Hard gig to fuck up."

"You'd think so. I got fired this afternoon."

"Congratulations," said Quick.

"Thank you," said Thackeray, grinning. A comfortable silence fell. Finally, Thackeray turned to Clay. "Well, my man, are you going to explain what the hell is happening here?"

"Thought you'd never ask." Clay stood up on the topmost support bar of the letter. Thackeray and Quick reached to steady him.

Clay waved them off. "Don't worry about me. And don't worry about yourselves either. As you may have noticed, we're in a different place. A place where both you guys exist at the same time."

"Where are we, exactly?" asked Quick.

"And where've we been?" seconded Thackeray.

"Let's take a little walkabout," suggested Clay.

"Walkabout?" Quick shook his head.

"Like this," said Clay, stepping off into the void. But he didn't fall. He just slid out calmly, standing in the air as if it were an invisible plane. He looked back, smiled. "Come on. Both of you. You can do it."

Gingerly each slid out a tentative foot, but it did not require faith to proceed. It was easy. It was stable.

"Now try this," said Clay, pushing off with both feet, a Superman push-off without the little run.

It worked. And now all three, in the grip of a gentle momentum, set off together, flying slowly without movement of limb.

It was the singlemost delightful feeling Quick had ever experienced. His body was instantly at home and comfortable. Like he was doing something long practiced but forgotten.

Thackeray felt exactly the same way. "Out-fucking-rageous." He'd done this before, he was positive.

They were drifting south, high over the Scientology Mansion, over Hollywood Boulevard, over the Hollywood Freeway. There was no fear. It was as natural as breathing.

"What happened to you guys is that you exchanged places," explained Clay. "In different universes, both of you jumped off the sign at the same time."

That made as much sense as anything. Thackeray looked over at Quick. "What did you do over there?"

"Well, earlier tonight, I won eleven Academy

Awards."

Thackeray was puzzled. "Eleven? Sounds like it was fixed."

"It was."

"Of course, it was." He had to laugh. It meant his long-term contract with Imperial was still in force. Bubbles Four through Twelve. He tried to think of something beautiful instead. "How's Thackstone?"

"Just as you left it. Couldn't find much to improve. It's a lovely place. I enjoyed it. And Ginger, uh," how would he put this, "Ginger is Ginger."

"You sleep with her?"

Quick was a little embarrassed. "Uh, yes I did." The truth seemed the best course.

"That's okay," said Thackeray. "I would've. And I don't mind." A pause. "Though I didn't sleep with Estelle."

"It would have been fine with me."

Thackeray smiled. "God bless Estelle anyway. She's a true friend. You know she's going to be angry with you."

"What now?

"Being fired from Grigson again."

"I quit last time. What happened?"

"Andrei came back."

"Really. From where?"

"From the paper-slipper ward at County/USC. Where I did a couple of weeks. Where I kept telling them I wasn't Michael Quick."

"I was at St. Martin's-By-The-Sea."

"Nice place. Where they told you *you* were Linden Thackeray."

"I finally agreed with them."

"When?"

"When I was told I was worth twenty-three million

dollars." Thackeray laughed aloud. "I would've done the same thing. By the way, you've gotten pretty famous yourself lately."

"*Me?* Michael Quick?"

"Michael Quick."

"Why?"

"*The Tides of Piss.*"

"Wow. I'd almost forgotten. Made me famous?"

"The Valley Theater League Awards. You won. Then there was a riot. And things built up from there."

Now Quick was puzzled. He given Andy McCulla permission to run with the Tides. But he'd never heard anything. He'd never heard of the Valley Theater League Awards, either. But he vaguely remembered writing something tidal. Maybe it was the Neil Cassidy/ Jack Kerouac amphetamine experiment. "You're sure about this?"

"Oh, I'm sure," said Thackeray. "Your anti-war shot across the bow."

"People liked it?"

"The reaction was strong on both sides. I was shot at this afternoon because of it." Thackeray touched his hairline. "Fucker ran a groove right down my scalp."

The trio passed over Wilshire Boulevard at Fairfax. Clay headed right, following the Miracle Mile westward.

Quick looked down, pointed out Sizzler. "That's where I broke up with Estelle on Christmas Eve."

Thackeray laughed. "She mentioned that in passing. What were you thinking?"

"I hadn't planned anything. Things just came to a head there. I was talking about Sizzler's next-best concept. You can't get something for nothing – but you can get a lot for a little."

"And by the time you get a little of this and a little of that you may as well have gone to the Palm to begin with. Those Sizzler thieves charge for butter."

Quick smiled a broad smile. "That's exactly it. And that's about what I said. Really pissed her off."

They floated in blessed silence for another miraculous minute, passing over La Cienega into Beverly Hills. Thackeray turned to Clay. "Why do Michael and I resemble one another?"

Clay grinned. "It's more than a resemblance, young brothers. You're identical in every way."

"And our fingerprints, seemingly, too," said Quick.

"Your fingerprints, too," said the Necessary Events Facilitator. He thought for a second. He had never explained this before. And he probably would never have to again. Most humans had no need to know. That's why he had chosen to be a thousand feet in air when the question was asked. To bolster the believability quotient. "To put it simply, both of you share the same soul. So you share identical bodies."

There was a long, long silence. Quick and Thackeray stared at one another.

"Bullshit," said Quick.

"Total bullshit," said Thackeray.

"It's not as strange as you think," continued Clay. "Christianity honors the triune god."

"So what?" Thackeray shook his head. The Father, the Son, the Holy Spirit. What did that really mean in the real world? If a person wasn't just himself, then all bets were off.

"Who cares about triune, Clay?" Quick found himself angry."Anyhow, there's two of us."

"Try to remember you're flying as we speak." The trio had reached the Wilshire/Santa Monica Boulevard split, turned south down Wilshire toward Santa Monica. "And just a point of interest here," added Clay, with celestial calm, "there are three of you."

"*THREE?*" Thackeray and Quick, electrified.

"The triune spirit. Successful for a reason. Each independent, but all One. Replicated throughout time and space. Triune beings all over the place."

"Why three?" Thackeray looked down. He *was* flying.

Clay shrugged. "I guess He liked it that way." He grinned. "Actually, He's Sevenfold."

"Oh, come on." Quick chuckled.

"Explain sevenfold," said Thackeray.

"It's arithmetic. First, He is One."

"Okay," said Quick.

"He is also Three."

Thackeray spread his hands. "And?"

"Well, three and one make Four. And there's the last combinations. Father and Son, that's Five. Father and Spirit, that's Six. Son and Spirit, Seven. Simple."

"Who is our triune third?" asked Thackeray.

"James Kirchoffer is the third member of the trio. A good man. Like both of you. In his different spacetime, he lives in New Chicago."

"I've never heard of New Chicago," said Quick.

"That's because it isn't here."

"Will we ever meet him?" Thackeray felt the beginning of a curiosity that would tickle him the rest of his days.

Clay shook his head. "Not even remotely possible. Both of *you* shouldn't have met. But here we are."

"How's Mr. Kirchoffer doing?" asked Quick.

"He's doing fine. He's a chief in the Navy."

They flew on. "Do we get to go back to where we came from?" Quick suddenly yearned for all the little things that had made his life his own.

"That's up to the both of you. It would be nice if you both agreed."

Quick looked into Thackeray's eyes. Communication ensued. He turned to Clay. "We agree." He looked down. Somehow they were over the Hollywood Hills again. There was the Hollywood sign. He turned to his twin again. "By the way, there's a girl you should meet. Her name's Leslie. You'd like her. In fact, you might come to love her. I did."

"Love is a strong word," said Thackeray.

"Love is the only word," said Clay.

"Where do I find her?" asked Thackeray.

"Her address is on your desk. There's just one catch."

"What's that?"

"Franklin."

"Who's Franklin?

"Franklin is a dude who followed her home. Now he's living there."

"Don't worry about Franklin," said Clay.

"Why shouldn't he?" asked Quick. "The dude followed her home."

"Well, because Franklin is a dog."

Quick found himself laughing, but he was pissed at the same time. "You, who can do anything, didn't think it was important to tell me that?"

"Not my job," said the NEF. "But you could've told him that," said Thackeray, loyal. "Could I meet this lady back in my world, Clay?"

Clay shrugged. "Anything's possible."

Quick was annoyed. "Can't you just tell us what the plan is? What you've really been doing?"

Clay attempted to put the meaning of everything in something as incredibly inefficient as human speech. It just wasn't possible. He spread his hands, almost helplessly. "Each of you signed up, exactly, for what you're going through. And at the same time, you create the future as you move through it."

That satisfied no one. Thackeray spoke up. "Is there a reason our wires got crossed?"

"Of course there's a reason."

"And that reason is—" prompted Quick.

"Putty," said Clay.

"Putty?" asked Thackeray.

"As in *Grigson Putty?"* asked Quick.

Clay nodded. "It's like this." Clay fondly looked at two of his three charges and sent the thought to each that would subtly pierce their special buoyancy. "Andrei Konaslavsky must and will repair the Looga Brothers Measured Filling Machine. However, he'll make a significant improvement that will make the runs of putty slightly more viscous than previous runs. One of the cans of the more viscous putty will fall into the path of a vehicle where it will split open faster than a less viscous can might. That little moment will save a life. A life that will become very important to life in the multiverse."

"Putty," said Thackeray.

"Putty," said Clay.

Thackeray turned to Quick, shrugged.

Quick shrugged in return. A thought struck him. Thackeray was a nice guy. "Hey. If you want to do something with the *Bubbles in the Tub* stuff you're welcome to it. Maybe you could make some money."

"And if you could use any of my efforts, I barely remember *Tides of Piss,* go right ahead."

"I liked *Zanen's Grave.* And *The Eagle and the Dove."*

"They're yours."

"Thank you, Michael," said Thackeray. "It was nice being mistaken for someone important."

Then Quick remembered Black Thursday. "And one more thing. I hope this doesn't cause you too much trouble."

"What did you do?"

"I tried to fire all the employees of Thackeray Entertainment. When I couldn't stop *Bubbles in the Tubbles*. Sorry."

Linden snorted. "Don't be sorry. The Bubbles train can't be stopped. As I'm sure you found out."

"You don't want to do it, either?"

"I don't. But it's written in stone. And I wrote it in stone."

Neither Quick nor Thackeray realized they were slowly sinking from the heavens. They were down to their last moments together.

"So, Clay," began Thackeray, "triune lives, quantum universes and all. What's the point? Why? Why? Why?"

Clay shrugged. "Why? I don't know. Just know what I've heard."

"Aren't you a NEF? They don't tell you things?" Quick was sure Clay knew everything.

"I'm not that important," said Clay. "My mission is a small one. To assist you, Linden, and James in the commission of your duties. But I'll tell you what I've heard."

"Tell us," said Thackeray.

Clay started in. "It's like this. All our lives, consecutive and simultaneous—"

But that was the last conscious moment Quick and Thackeray were in common spacetime. The next moment, each, in his universe of birth, plummeted from the Hollywood sign to the earth below.

Chapter 43

Quick Makes a Deal

Quick never remembered hitting the ground, just waking up to an unknown face barely visible behind a blinding flashlight.

"This asshole's alive," said the uniformed man to unseen others. He redirected his attention back to Quick. "Let me guess. You didn't win an Academy Award so you jumped off the sign. And then your shitty old Cadillac gets towed. What a night."

Quick smiled up at the stranger with perfect happiness. His Cadillac. He was back.

A week later, based on his *Tides of Piss* notoriety and chutzpah from an alternate universe, he wangled a mid-morning appointment with the head of National Studios, Arnon Faubus.

"You've caused quite a stir around here," said Faubus, lighting a cigar. "Is it true you were working downtown at a putty factory?"

Quick spread his hands. "Research is research, what can I say. And it's honest work, besides. But I've got something great for you."

"It isn't about putty, is it?"

"Putty is more significant than you think. But no, it isn't about putty."

"Good. What's it about?"

"It's about sex, drugs, and flatulence. And hot tubs. It's a low, low, low comedy. I call it *Bubbles in the Tub.*

"Bubbles in the Tub." Faubus slapped the surface of his desk, rose to his feet, his mood leavened with

optimism and relief. "I thought you were going to bring me some heavy shit. But this is right down my alley. No heavy message stuck in there for the good of us all?"

"No message whatsoever. Just fun. No Academy Award potential whatsoever."

Faubus smiled. "Then count me in."

"I want a million dollars," said Quick, talking through his ass.

Faubus shrugged. "Fine."

"And I'll want my own production company."

"Okay."

"And office space."

"Of course."

Quick left Faubus' office a rich man. Right before the elevator he heard a voice calling him. He turned. And there was Leslie. Or at least a woman absolutely identical to Leslie.

"Yes?"

"I've read a few of your scripts, Mr. Quick. Maybe one day we can talk about *The Eagle and the Dove*."

"Okay. Let's talk about it tonight."

The lovely girl shrugged, half embarrassed. "Alright."

Quick smiled at her, riding a beam of perfect confidence and happiness. "Whom do I have the pleasure of addressing?"

"My name is Caroline. Caroline Evers."

"Where do you live, Caroline?"

"Melrose."

"Perfect. Eight o'clock, Angel Café."

Caroline chirped out a little laugh. "You're on."

Quick pointed. "No, you're on."

Caroline was studying him, a curious expression on her face. "Have we met?"

"Yes," said Quick, "but don't ask me when."

"I'll see you tonight."

"Eight o'clock, Angel Café."

Quick waved. Caroline waved. Quick waved again. Caroline smiled, waved again. Things were almost sticky.

Quick checked his watch, decided he would cut the Gordian Knot. "What about lunch, too? Right now?"

Caroline laughed. "You're a fast worker."

Later that glorious afternoon, after he had dropped her back off at National, Quick drove downtown to Grigson. He saw his replacement, the famous and essential Andrei, lidding one-pound cans with style and aplomb. That's how it's done, thought Quick.

Then Ed Strickman walked in. If Quick hadn't known better, the floor supervisor radiated some kind of embarrassment. "Hi, Michael," he said.

"Hey, Ed. How's it hanging?"

Strickman's genital piercing was a total secret. It had been accomplished in San Francisco, the most daring act of his life. What did Quick really mean? How could he possibly know? Quick didn't even look mad over the firing. "Things are, uh, cool," said Strickman, using the word for the very first time. "What can I do for you? Can you mix? You're not looking for a position, are you?"

"Nah. I'm wondering if Clay is around."

Strickman shook his head. "Clay quit. This morning. Didn't come in. Just a phone call. We're looking for somebody."

"Someone'll turn up."

Strickman nodded. "They always do."

"Well, I'm outa here, then," said Quick, "stay cool."

Strickman looked after the departing Quick. The son of a bitch was a writer after all.

Chapter 44

Thackeray Gets it Right

Linden Thackeray didn't remember his fall either. He awoke with a headache and a backache. He guessed he'd passed the night on the mountain. Like Moses. He stumbled down the steep slopes of Hollywoodland, found himself on Beachwood Avenue. Eventually he came to the small business district. He saw his reflection in the glass of a coffee shop. He looked like shit. Coffee could help. He had just ordered when he heard a reverent, if tentative, voice. "Congratulations, Mr. Thackeray."

Mr. Thackeray. He was filled with a golden happiness. Maybe this was the universe where he had won ten awards. Or eleven. Whatever. He looked around. "Thank you. Thank you, very much."

"You're welcome. You won a lot of awards last night."

Thackeray looked at her, smiled. "I guess I did. And it looks like you celebrated for me."

"I did. It was hell of a party. And you. You look like you slept in the bushes."

Thackeray laughed a booming laugh. "I may have. It was one of those parties, too."

"I met you at a party just like that."

"You did?"

"You were pretty hammered. At Jean Harlow's house. In Whitley Heights." The girl stuck out her hand. "I'm Candy Lee Jopsie. Would you like to come to my place and freshen up? I live right around the corner."

Some people were born luckier than others, Thackeray mused later. He had been back in the local universe less than twelve hours and he'd already met an insatiable acrobat.

Perhaps Quick had been equally fortunate. Certainly he wished his secret sharer well. There was a wry comfort in his existence. *Buona fortuna,* Michael.

That evening, after he had banished Dr. Boother and Ginger from Thackstone, he drove down to Melrose and knocked at the address left on his desk.

A pretty, dark-haired girl answered the door. "Michael!" she shrieked, running into his arms. His tempered response alerted her to something odd. She stepped back, looked into his eyes, said nothing. Then she spoke. "Are you, Michael? You're *not* Michael, are you?"

"I'm—"

"You're Linden Thackeray. The real Linden Thackeray."

"Yes. Am I addressing the chess champion?"

"Where is he?"

"Where's Michael? Back in the world he came from."

"Where he's really Michael."

"Where he's really Michael."

"Can you explain?"

"I could try. It's a mouthful."

A dog appeared behind her legs, looking up at him. "That must be Franklin."

"Michael told you?"

"He thought Franklin was a man."

"Oh, nooo." She recalled Michael's last phone call. With the sad, inexplicable ending. "What else did Michael tell you?"

Thackeray looked, really looked, into her eyes. "He said that he loved you. And if I got to know you, I might, too. If I was really, really lucky."

Leslie really looked at Thackeray. Studied him. "Are you a good man?" Thackeray felt an unseen gate opening before him. "I could be. I could be better."

There was a long pause. Then Leslie smiled. "Want to walk down to Canter's, get a sandwich or something?"

"That'd be perfect."

"Call me Leslie."

"That'd be perfect, Leslie."

Chapter 45

To Illuminate the Heavens and Warm the Feet of God

Back in the universe that had spawned him, on the National lot, Quick hurried to his completely refurbished 1969 Cadillac Coupe de Ville. It was starting to rain and Caroline was waiting at Book Soup. Once behind the wheel, he leaned in to start the vehicle but dropped the keys onto the new carpeting.

Reaching for them, he rammed his forehead into the very cool steering ball that he had added to the steering wheel. Bringing his hand to impact point with a curse, Quick suddenly remembered Clay's complete last words concerning the reason humans were created.

At that same instant, at Thackstone, doing the backstroke, Thackeray miscalculated and rammed the back of his head into the Mexican tiling. Suddenly he recalled Clay's complete last words concerning the reason humans were created.

"It's like this," Clay had begun. "All our lives, consecutively and simultaneously triune, stretched over time, in concert with the lives of all other sentient, self-aware creatures, together form a tapestry of experience and perfection."

"That's a mouthful," said Quick.

"Yeah, yeah, yeah," said Thackeray. "But what's the tapestry *for?*"

Clay, who had been a NEF since the first instant of creation, smiled broadly. Life was very, very good.

And there was a lot of it. "The purpose of the tapestry, my children," said Clay in a low, clear voice, "is to illuminate the heavens. To illuminate the heavens and warm the feet of God."

Clay's deep, mellifluous laugh vibrated through the multiverse. And then it was gone.

The End

EPILOGUE ONE

Legit Review **Tides of Piss** *Los Angeles*
By Howard Densmore
An Oxford Theatre production of a play in three acts by Linden Thackeray, directed by David Paul David. 99 seats, $40.

Abandoning all he was ever good at, one of Hollywood's best screenwriters, Linden Thackeray, exposes himself, witlessly delving into the Iraq War with two clumsy boots in this execrable, over-the-top, three act play. Left of the far, far left, an emotional hodge-podge devoid of skill and reason, a worthless evening is guaranteed for all. Whither go ye, Linden Thackeray?

EPILOGUE TWO

Business Top Story
Thack Sacked
Former tent-pole director fired
By Howard Densmore

Linden Thackeray, 12-time Oscar winner, has been fired by Imperial Studios following the unapologetic production of his universally panned play, ***The Tides of Piss****. Charlie Finkster, Imperial prexy, has released Thackeray from his long-term contract. "America speaks, I listen," said Finkster. The remainder of the* ***Bubbles in the Tub*** *franchise (4-12) has been canceled as well.*

p.g. sturges

p.g. sturges makes his home in Portland, Oregon. An autodidact, he's been a submarine sailor, a Christmas tree farmer, a metrologist, an author, a screenwriter, a playwright, and a musician. As a songwriter, he remains the only known connection between David Lee Roth and Barry Manilow.

Sturges and his wife, Paige, own and operate Barking Lion, publisher of this and other novels.

Made in the USA
Monee, IL
26 May 2022